The Cheater

By Ruby Reverte

Chapter 1

Detention

Amaryllis put her mathematics textbook inside her locker and looked in the small square mirror located on its tiny door. She checked her makeup and her hair, pushing her blonde hair behind her shoulders and away from her face.

Reaching inside her pink bag, she took out her 'Pink in the Afternoon' lipstick by Revlon and applied some on her small lips. Just as she finished applying her lipstick, she heard someone calling her name. She closed her locker door and turned around, only to find her best friend running toward her and stumbling more times than she could count. Rose came to a sudden stop in front of Amaryllis. She bent down slightly with her hands on her knees and panted heavily, her frizzy hair falling all over her face.

"You...c-come quickly...Nate and Derek... fighting," she managed to wheeze out.

Amaryllis' eyes widened and she grabbed Rose by the hand and ran down the school hallway. The hallway had blue walls and a marble white and black floor. The hallway was filled with lockers that were also blue and had golden handles.

Once Amaryllis and Rose reached the end of the hallway, they turned left and continued running until they came in front of a pair of double doors. They tore the doors open and rushed inside, pushing through the crowd that had formed around the centre of the dining room. There were plates half full of roast chicken and mashed potatoes on the dining tables, and glasses were filled with lingonberry juice, but all the chairs were empty. Big chandeliers hung from the high ceiling and there were rectangular windows that were covered with black curtains. The curtains managed to block most of the sunlight that tried to come in. If it was not for the wind that occasionally pushed the curtains aside, thereby letting some sunlight escape inside, no one would know it was daylight.

"Fight, fight, fight," the crowd chanted.

Some students clapped, some students whistled but all students cheered the fight on.

"Hey, watch it," a girl screamed as Amaryllis pushed her aside, Rose following behind her by a couple of steps. Rose had her head ducked down as she followed Amaryllis through the crowd. Finally, they made it to the centre of the room. There, two men or perhaps they should be referred to as two boys were standing in front of each other, panting as they had just run a marathon.

One boy had blonde hair with dull blue eyes and big cheeks that hung down his face. He wore a tie that was navy and sloppy around his neck and navy trousers. His white shirt had a missing arm and it certainly was not because he was experimenting with his uniform. Only the girls did that. Sometimes they cut both arms of their shirt to make a vest and sometimes they dyed their tie pink. Despite getting detention for a month and a three-hour lecture delivered by the principal herself, they couldn't seem to stop changing their boring uniforms. Or, maybe they just didn't want to.

The other boy, however, had hair the colour of the night with piercing blue eyes that looked like they had all the oceans of the world in them. They sparkled with all the lighter shades of blue that could be found in the sky on a sunny morning. His jaw looked like it could cut through glass and his skin was clearer than the full moon when it shone in the night sky.

God clearly had favourites.

This boy had managed to keep both arms of his shirt intact, but the same could not be said about his tie which lay ripped on the floor. Amaryllis watched the scene in front of her with her mouth wide open. Just as she moved toward the two boys, the blonde boy screamed and landed a punch on the other boy's face. Perhaps he thought he was in a war movie where you had to scream when you attacked someone. The victim screamed as his once-perfect face was now bruised with a red mark that was slowly turning blue. The victim landed a kick on the boy's stomach, causing him to scream in pain and stumble to the ground. He got up in no time, and they both screamed as they tried to lunge at each other once again.

"That's enough," Amaryllis screamed as she stood in between them and pushed them away from each other. There was a moment of silence as they stopped their fighting and shifted their attention to her then back to each other. For a second, one would have thought that they recognised how stupid they looked and that they would be sensible. That they would end the fight and walk away from each other. Instead, the opposite happened. At the same time, as if rehearsed, they both attempted to pounce on each other. Amaryllis anticipated this as her hands shot out from her sides, pushing them away before they could achieve their goal.

"Stop it. You are acting like children," she said.

"He started it," the blonde boy said in his soft voice.

"You're pointing fingers like a five-year-old child," the dark-haired beauty retorted at the same time.

Amaryllis threw her pink handbag behind her and turned to look at them both, "I don't care who started it. All I want is to get through my last year of high school without drama. Now stop this before Mrs Smith comes and we all get detention for the rest of our lives." The two boys shot each other one last dirty look
before retreating and starting to pick up their belongings from the floor. There was a tie, a shirt, a sleeve and two black shoulder bags on the floor. The bags were open and papers, textbooks and pens were scattered around the floor. The blonde boy tried to pick up the last thing left, his shirt sleeve. He picked it up, left it, and then picked it up again. He was probably thinking about what he would do with it. After all, it's not like he would have it sewn back onto his shirt. Of course not, how preposterous! No, he would buy a new shirt even though it cost two hundred pounds. Only peasants would care about such things to save money. But not the students that went to this private school. These students lived in big mansions, had their private drivers and were worth at least a few millions before they were born.

This was one of the most prestigious private schools in England. Only the richest of the rich could afford to send their children here. It cost millions of pounds to attend every year. The school prided itself on its outstanding teaching and diversity. The students were all British but were all from different ethnic backgrounds, although most were white.

Out of the blue, a clapping sound echoed throughout the big dining room. All heads turned to where the sound had come from and there, sitting on one of the tables was a girl with flawless porcelain skin and brown hair that cascaded down in loose curls. Her clapping came to an end and she jumped off the table, taking slow strides towards what was a second ago a fight scene.

She stopped near the dark-haired boy and ran her hand down his muscly arm, "Derek," she acknowledged him with a flirtatious look. Amaryllis rolled her eyes at this and crossed her arms, glaring at the girl. "Nate," she said, not even sparing a glance at the blonde, whose cheeks turned a rosy colour at the mention of his name.

The girl came to a stop a few feet in front of Amaryllis, "always toying around with the boys, are we?" Amaryllis glared harder at her and crossed her fingers behind her back, wishing she would just leave her alone when she doesn't give her the reaction she craves. Usually, this would work but today she couldn't be more wrong. The bell rang, indicating the beginning of the next lesson, causing the crowd of students to rush out of the dining room. The only people that were left were Derek, Nate, Rose, Amaryllis and the troublemaker, also known as Isabel.

Isabel took a few more steps towards Amaryllis, nearly closing the gap between them so that they were only a few inches apart, "what's wrong? Cat got your tongue... slut?" she said, emphasising the last word with a click of her tongue. Amaryllis stared at her with a straight face. She took a deep breath in and then breathed out. She hoped her face would lose some of its now red colour, but the redness only intensified.

Suddenly she grabbed Isabel's hair and pulled it.

Hard.

Isabel screamed like a cat that had its tail stepped on. She tried to drag Amaryllis' hands off her hair, but it was as if Amaryllis' hands were glued to her hair. Amaryllis tangled her fingers in Isabel's locks whilst Isabel grabbed Amaryllis' blonde hair and yanked it with force. Amaryllis screamed as she tackled her to the ground and straddled her. Isabel's hands left Amaryllis' hair and tried to push Amaryllis off her. She pounded her fists on Amaryllis' chest but it was of no use. Amaryllis kept her iron grip and continued pulling her hair. Nate attempted to pull Amaryllis off Isabel, but she used one hand and pushed him away. He stumbled and fell backwards with a thud. Rose, on the other hand, was cheering her best friend on and telling her to 'pull her hair and ruin those perfect locks that she didn't deserve.' Meanwhile, Derek had his phone out and was filming the entire scene. He even made sure to zoom in on Nate falling after Amaryllis pushed him.

"What on earth is happening here?" a voice boomed, echoing throughout the dining room and making the portraits on the walls shake.

Derek hid his phone faster than the speed of lightning. Rose stopped her cheering, her hands paused mid-air as if this was a movie someone had pressed the pause button on. Amaryllis and Isabel stopped fighting. Amaryllis got off Isabel and tried to fix her hair by running her hands through it, whilst Isabel got up and straightened her navy skirt and fixed her tie. The headteacher walked dangerously slowly towards her misbehaving students and took a couple of seconds to glare at every one of them, her gaze lingering on Amaryllis the longest.

"Derek, Rose, Nate, Amaryllis and Isabel, you have all earned yourself a two-hour detention this evening after school," the headteacher said.

She dismissed everyone with a wave of her hand but told Amaryllis and Isabel to stay. They looked like two chickens who had been in a fight. Their hair was messy and all over the place, and their uniforms looked like messy pyjamas that they had worn to bed.

"I am so disappointed in you two, especially you Miss Knight. I expected better from an A student," the headteacher said the last bit whilst narrowing her eyes at Amaryllis.

Amaryllis bowed her head down in shame whilst Isabel rolled her eyes. The headteacher was a petite woman with big broad shoulders and a stomach that screamed I have been eating pasta all week. Her high temper sure did not match her petite frame. She was known to snap at any questions asked by students which she classified as stupid. This happened all the time since any questions asked were classified as stupid by her. She was also known to snap at any little thing that wasn't perfect.

An ideal example would be someone's tie not being tight enough around their neck. One day she came into an English lesson to inspect her students. She noticed that one of the boys had a sloppy tie and so she started to tighten it around his neck. She kept tightening it until the poor boy's face turned yellow. He grew dizzy and had to be quickly taken to the school nurse.

The headteacher's sense of fashion was as strict as her personality. She always wore a black pencil skirt with a blue shirt and a navy blazer. Some students joked that she might think she had a uniform since she always wore the same outfit each day.

"I will have a conversation with your mother today," Mrs Smith said.

Amaryllis' eyes nearly bulged out from her face, "can't you have a conversation with my father when he comes back from his trip?"

The headteacher gave her a look that said 'are you telling me what to do' and then dismissed them both. As they exited the dining room Isabel had a smug smile across her face whilst Amaryllis looked like she was Satan and was being sent to hell for eternal damnation.

Amaryllis had her head down and was writing on a piece of paper that had all kinds of mathematical equations on it. She only tore her eyes away from her page when she opened her textbook and flickered through the pages, scanning her eyes through the familiar symbols and the equations. Rose on the other hand was filing her nails and humming a happy rhythm as if she was on vacation not in detention. Isabel had her head rested on her hand and only stopped looking dreamily at Derek to shoot Rose a glare, "you're destroying my ears, shut up." But Rose just hummed louder in response.

Derek sat on his chair, glaring at the poor teacher with a murderous gaze. The teacher was sitting at the front desk. He gulped whenever Derek glared at him and kept looking at the time, probably wanting the detention to end even more than the students themselves. The clock read 4:30 pm. There were still thirty minutes left. There was one student in particular who did not care how many minutes of detention were left. That student was Nate. Nate, oh Nate who was snoring loudly in his chair. He had his head thrown back, making it look like his neck would snap if he just bent his head down an inch more. Derek would occasionally kick his chair and Nate would snap his eyes open, wipe the drool hanging from the side of his mouth with the one sleeve he had left, and fall back asleep again. After several times of waking him up, Derek gave up and never bothered to assault his chair again. Instead, he turned his attention to his next victim.

"Psst, princessa, pssst," Derek called Amaryllis. He sat on a chair that was one chair to the left of hers and one row behind hers. Amaryllis stuffed her cotton balls further inside her ears and continued scribbling things down on her textbook. With a pink pen, she scribbled down $y = mx + c$. She shut her textbook and finished filling in her page full of mathematical questions including questions about equations and vectors. She hissed when something kicked her chair from behind. She slammed her pen down and put the piece of paper inside her textbook. Taking her cotton balls out, she turned around and glared at Derek.

"What do you want?" she hissed.

"You," he said with a smirk plastered across his face.

"Fuck you."

"You wish."

"Ugh."

"Let me take you out on a date princessa. Our last date was so short."

"You only get one chance and you screwed yours over," she said and turned her back to him, but not before seeing his smirk fall. As she continued to do her mathematics work, she could feel two pairs of eyes staring at her. She instantly knew whom they belonged to because of how they made her feel. One made her feel angry and the other made her feel even angrier if that was possible.

Walking down the steps of the school, Amaryllis and Rose had already started to plan the rest of their glamorous day. They were busy laughing and talking whilst the rest of their detention crew walked gloomily past them. Derek stole a glance at Amaryllis, who didn't even look in his direction.

A big black car came and a driver with a black suit, black hat and black sunglasses stepped out of the car and opened the door to Amaryllis and Rose. They went inside the car and Amaryllis told the driver to take them to the shopping centre. He informed her that her mother expected her to be home as soon as her detention finished, but she was not in the mood for another one of her mother's lectures. She had already had enough drama for one day. She just wanted to have a nice time with her best friend.

As the driver drove by the streets of England, many beautiful sights could be seen. Further away from the busyness of the streets and cars, a pink bridge could be spotted. It had a lake underneath it and there was a mother duck swimming with her seven little ducklings. The mother duck came out of the water
and shook her leg dry. She then preceded to walk on the bridge and crossed to the grass area in the small park. Her children imitated their mother by shaking their legs and crossing the bridge.

On the other side of the road, there were several famous restaurants where celebrities could always be spotted visiting. One of Amaryllis' favourite restaurants was the pink one on 7th avenue street. It was a French restaurant, famous for its mouth-watering stakes, cheeses and French toast dishes that were served for dessert. Next to it was the French bakery, La Rose.

"Stop here and then you can continue to the shopping centre," Amaryllis said to her driver who just nodded curtly.

La Rose was all pink from the outside. The door and the windows were all pink, and there were a few white chairs and white tables outside if people wanted to get fresh air whilst enjoying their dessert. Pink peonies decorated the windows and the door, making it look like something from a fairy tale. As soon as they entered, a bell rang and they could smell the freshly baked goods - they could smell the strawberries, the chocolate, the waffles and the cream. There was a chocolate fountain next to the entrance and there was a queue where you had to wait to order. The queue was always long and after about forty-five minutes of waiting, it was their turn to order.

"Can I have a French toast with strawberries, dark chocolate and cream please," Amaryllis said, handing the cashier her card. The cashier swiped her card and handed it back to Amaryllis.

"Can I please have two chocolate macarons and a waffle with cream and milk chocolate on top," Rose said and handed her card to the cashier. She blushed when he made eye contact. Amaryllis flashed her a mischievous smile. The cashier swiped her card and then frowned. Rose watched his expression and her and Amaryllis exchanged confused looks. He swiped it again and the card machine flashed a red light.

"Sorry mademoiselle it seems your card has been stopped," he said with a heavy French accent and handed the card back to Rose, whose face was now flushed red.

If anyone saw her face, they would have thought she had painted her face red. Her hands shook as she looked for some cash in her brown purse. She only found a fifty-pound note and a ten-pound which made the total sixty pounds. Thankfully, that was the total of her order.

She extended her hand to give it to the cashier who shook his head, "sorry we only accept card payments."

Rose gave Amaryllis a desperate look but Amaryllis had already reached for her card and given it to the cashier, "here, put it on my card."

Deeper inside the Bakery, there were tables and chairs. The tables were round and small, some were pink, and some were white. The plates that the pastries and desserts were served on were surprisingly green. The green plates had tiny pink flowers on them that complimented the pink design of the cafe. Amaryllis and Rose made their way to their usual table, in the middle of the room. This had been their table ever since they first came to La Rose three years ago.

Once they had settled into their seats, Rose put her head in her hands whilst Amaryllis stroked her arm to comfort her. After a few deep breaths, Rose put her hands down and turned to Amaryllis, "we're probably going to get bankrupt again," she said and sniffed, tears starting to form in her eyes.

"Don't say that. I am sure there has been some kind of mistake," Amaryllis said, a look of sympathy coating her features.

"Why do these things only happen to me? They never happen to you or anyone else," Rose complained whilst tears streamed down from her big brown eyes. Amaryllis opened her mouth to say something but closed it when the waitress came over with their dessert. Maybe it would be best to just let Rose calm down by herself, she thought. The waitress put down a plate of French toast in front of Amaryllis and a small plate of two macarons in front of Rose as well as a big plate of waffles with cream and chocolate. Amaryllis thanked the waitress and took in the heavenly smell. For the rest of their time there, they both ate mostly in silence, not opening their mouths besides to say how delicious the food was.

After they finished their food, Rose rushed home to speak to her mother. Whereas, Amaryllis had decided to skip her shopping trip and head straight home. She arrived at the mansion where she lived. It was a big white mansion with rose bushes decorating its sides and a water fountain in front of it. She knocked on the door and waited a couple of seconds.

"Weird, did Mrs Thomas leave early?" she muttered to herself as she reached inside her bag for her keys. Her keys jingled as she inserted them into the door lock. After a small fight with the door lock, she was inside. She hung her bag on the hook on the wall. Taking off her socks, she threw them in the basket full of dirty clothes near the door. Her bare feet came in contact with the cold stair surface as she planned to make her way to her room.

She tiptoed up the stairs and sighed when she felt her feet come in contact with the warm surface of the rug on the second floor. As she was about to turn right to go to her room she heard a murmuring noise from the guest room. Had her mother's sister come to visit? Or perhaps her dad was back from his trip early and decided to once again sleep in the guest room. She skipped happily to the room, hoping to see her dad but her body abruptly came to a stop and her face fell in disappointment. The door was open slightly and she saw her mother standing there.

"I missed you so much," she heard her mother's voice say and then a kissing sound followed. A smile spread across her face once again. This meant that her parents had finally made up from their recent fight. She prayed this would be the last of their fights.

She felt like jumping up and down from happiness until she heard a familiar voice say, "I haven't seen you in weeks" and her face fell again.

Chapter 2

That Man

Amaryllis' hands shook and her feet wanted to give way. She felt the room spin around her and put her hand on the wall to steady herself. For a moment she thought that she must be in a dream and this was when she woke up. The room just kept spinning faster and faster. She felt as if she was riding on a never-ending rollercoaster. She stumbled to the stairs and took slow steps downwards, careful not to fall. She sighed in relief as she reached the last few steps. Suddenly though, the room started spinning even faster and black dots clouded her vision. She blinked her eyes a couple of times but the black dots wouldn't go away as she stumbled down the last step. She gripped the handrail of the stairs and safely made it to the floor. She rushed as fast as she could to the living room and threw herself onto the safety of the cream couch. Stifling a sob, she curled her body into a ball as tears poured down her face like a waterfall. She made a fist and put it in her mouth so no one could hear her misery.

Footsteps could be heard going down the stairs and she quickly masked her miserable state by wiping her tears with the sleeves of her shirt and taking out her magic potion from her small shoulder bag. She had forgotten her bag on the couch the night before when she came back from having dinner with her mother. She applied a generous amount of her foundation on her cheeks and nose to make them look white again, instead of the pink they had turned into. After she was done concealing her misery, she rummaged through her bag, pretending like she was looking for something.

"Sweetheart I thought you texted me and said you would stay at Rose's today," her mother said, coming into the living room. Following her mother was that... man. He walked in smiling at Amaryllis as if he hadn't done a thing.

He went up to her and ruffled her hair, "hey kiddo." Amaryllis glared up at him. His smile fell and a frown replaced it, "what's wrong?" Amaryllis shifted her gaze to the floor as if it was the most interesting thing. She stood up and tossed her bag over her shoulder.

"Nothing am just tired," she said as she went past her mother and up the stairs for the second time today. Her mother and her lover stared after her with furrowed eyebrows. As soon as she was in her room, she stripped from her school clothes and got into the hot bath the maid prepared for her every day after school. She opened the wine bottle and poured herself a generous amount of pinot noir. She finished the glass and poured herself another glass, then another, to the point where she lost count of how many glasses she had drunk. But she had probably only drank a few glasses like two. Or maybe three. Maybe seven.

    Wrapping herself in a white towel, she made her way to the bathroom double doors and went through them to her princess bedroom. Her bed had a Victorian style white frame whilst her curtains and bedding were pink. Her pillowcases and her duvet cover were made from silk and they were a light shade of pink. She had a huge closet on the left side of the room. There was also a white desk that had all kinds of supplies a maths lover would have. Pencils, rulers, calculators, protractors and maths textbooks were scattered everywhere, as well as pi stickers. The desk had open shelves underneath and there you could glimpse the names of fashion magazines like Vogue and the names of many famous fashion books.

    Standing in front of her wardrobe, she took out a matching white bra and piece of underwear and slipped them on. She also pulled out a pink mini dress and slipped it on. It had a v neck and dainty little gems on the sides that were the same colour as the dress, making them almost invisible. Whenever those gems caught the light from the lightbulb in her room they glowed, making her dress look like it appeared from a fairy tale. She put on a pair of white flats and waved her blonde hair with her hair straightener. She edged closer to her full-length mirror that was standing tall near her closet and applied some purple eyeliner to accentuate her blue eyes and a bit of pink lip-gloss.

    The dining room had a big chandelier that hung over the dining table. The table had eight chairs surrounding it. Two on either end of the table and six on either side.

At dinner, Amaryllis sat in front of her mother's lover and her mother sat at the head of the table, where her father usually sat. If a pin dropped the sound would echo throughout the huge dining room. They ate in awkward silence, apart from the few times her mother's lover attempted to make one of his inappropriate jokes, but seeing as no one laughed he stopped and joined in the habit of eating in silence. Usually, her mother would tell her lover off whilst Amaryllis and her dad laughed so hard, that they thought their stomachs would explode. But not today. Not after what she'd witnessed. Amaryllis poked around the food on her plate. Her mother and her lover had nearly finished their stake and mashed potatoes. Half of their plates were also filled with steamed broccoli and carrots since her mother had always insisted on healthy eating.

For as long as she could remember, her mother had forced Amaryllis to finish her veggies, otherwise, she was not allowed to leave the dinner table. Amaryllis was only allowed dessert once a week. On her fifteenth birthday, her mother had pulled Amaryllis aside and told her that she could only eat a small slice of her birthday cake otherwise she would get sick and die. She had also explained to her that from now on she was only allowed a small portion of dessert once a week. At this stage, Amaryllis was surprised that she had not developed an eating disorder.

Oh, what her mother would do if she found out she visited La Rose daily. Her not getting an eating disorder was probably all thanks to her father who was the opposite of her mother and just let Amaryllis eat whatever she wanted. Whenever she used to crave dessert at night and text him from her bedroom, he used to sneak her some dessert from the kitchen after her mother was asleep. However, in the past few years, her father had not been there as much because of his frequent 'work' trips.

Amaryllis had eaten a few bites of her food and was now nibbling on a carrot. She occasionally glanced at the traitors from the corner of her eyes and saw them smiling at each other. Did they seriously think she didn't notice? Did they seriously think they could just fool around, and nobody would know? Suddenly, the doorbell rang, interrupting Amaryllis' angry thoughts.

"Are you expecting anyone?" the traitor asked her mother. Her mother shook her head as she swallowed her last bite. She got up and opened the door. Whoever was behind that door had caused her mother's face to turn yellow and her eyes to widen in shock.

Her next sentence almost made her lover choke on his broccoli, "darling you're back early," she faked the excitement in her voice. As always. Amaryllis could feel her mother's lover stiffen in his seat. He put his fork down and gulped some water. She shot him a wicked grin that he didn't quite catch as he was still drowning himself with his water.

He got up from his seat to greet the person he had known all his life. The person who always had his back. The person that always believed and supported him with everything he wanted to accomplish when no one else did. The person who had practically raised him. His brother.

He walked to his brother with arms wide open and gave his brother a big man hug. Amaryllis looked at her uncle in disgust, he was no longer the cool fun uncle that used to make her laugh, he was no longer her best friend. He was a traitor, and he was now a stranger. She did not know who he was anymore. The look of disgust was soon replaced with a look of confusion. How could she not have seen it before? The constant visits increased especially when her father was on a 'work' trip. The inside jokes he shared with her mother. All the time he or her mother would randomly text her and ask her if she was going to come home or stay at Rose's house. They were cheating and cheating in her house, in her father's house.

She came back to the present moment and got pulled out of her thoughts when she felt herself get engulfed in a big warm hug. A genuine hug, not like the rigid and awkward hug her uncle gave her dad. She wrapped her arms around the only man she now trusted and held on for dear life. She sighed. This was her only safe place.

"My baby girl I missed you so much," he said. I missed you so much. That sentence felt like a dagger piercing through her heart. That was the same sentence her mother said to her lover a few moments ago when she thought nobody would witness their infidelity. That traitor. Amaryllis mumbled something barely audible against her father's chest. Her father struggled to pull out of the hug as Amaryllis' arms only tightened around him. She clung to him like her life depended on it.

"What was that...look at you Amaryllis, you've grown so much since I last saw you," he said whilst smiling brightly after managing to tear her hands off him.

She couldn't help but laugh, "you saw me three days ago."

He loved calling her by her name instead of using endearing terms like sweetheart or darling. He had chosen her name himself and although he and his wife were English and Amaryllis was a Greek name, Richard loved the name so much that even Lisa could not stop him from naming his daughter Amaryllis.

"I want to see you eat at least half of your plate," her father said, pointing to her barely touched food. Amaryllis forced a smile and took a big bite of her steak and mashed potatoes. It tasted disgusting. It was laced with something odd. She could not quite put her finger around it, but then it dawned upon her. It was laced with betrayal. Speaking of betrayal, her mother and uncle looked like they had just come back from a funeral. Their faces looked drained of colour, and they stared into space. First Amaryllis disturbed their sinful night and then her father made a surprise return home. Her father's return was the icing on the cake. Poor love birds what bad luck. Maybe it was too late to say better luck next time because now her father was here and now their infidelity had to be put to an end. At least until her dad took another trip. Or so she thought.

"So... Mrs Smith called. She says you have been engaging in physical fights and hitting random people for no reason," her mother said, a stern look on her face. Amaryllis didn't even put her head up to meet her mother's intense gaze. She continued playing with her food. Tossing the broccoli from one side of the plate to the other. She hated broccoli.

"Answer me, child," her mother's calm tone fainted and was replaced by an angry tone.

"Calm down Lisa. Give her a chance to explain," Amaryllis' father said.

"Richard, stay out of this. You always let her do whatever she wants and look at what she's doing now. She is hitting people for god's sake. Next thing you know she might be jailed for violence," her mother frantically screamed.

"Firstly, the fight was only with one person, and they started it," Amaryllis said, holding her arms up defensively. Her mother rubbed her forehead with her fingers.

"I know this isn't going to go anywhere. You are never going to accept responsibility for what you have done," her mother said in disbelief.

Amaryllis put her hand on her mouth to stifle a laugh but by the look on her mother's face, she wasn't successful. Her mother glared at her, "you find this funny?" she asked, raising her voice even more.

"Enough," Richard said, raising his voice at his wife, silencing her. "As soon as I come home you start fighting with someone, with anyone you can find and now it's our daughter's turn?"

Lisa looked at her husband and managed to perfect her signature fake smile once again, "darling why don't you go and rest. You are probably exhausted from your long trip." Her father huffed and stood up from his chair. Her uncle whose name was James exchanged a smile with Lisa for what seemed to be the hundredth time today. Amaryllis' hands made a fist by her sides, and she clenched her mouth shut, preventing herself from saying anything she would regret. But it was too late.

"Just make sure to wash the bedsheets, they're really dirty," the words left her mouth before she could even process what she had said. Amaryllis stared at her mother and uncle and watched their expressions go from confused to nervous. Her uncle gulped down some more water whilst her mother watched her with weary eyes.

She gave her an uneasy smile, "what do you mean, darling?" Amaryllis paused for a moment, deciding whether to tell her father about his wife's affair with his brother. His blood.

"I accidentally spilt some juice on the bedsheets when I went into the room today." She decided against telling him. Lisa glanced at James and then back at her daughter who held her gaze, looking at her mother like the cheater that she was.

"Well, everyone, have a nice evening," James said, getting up from his seat.

"I will have to get going. I have to get up early tomorrow morning for work," he said, checking his wrist for his non-existent watch and patting Richard on the shoulder before heading for the door.

"No one asked," Amaryllis called out through gritted teeth. She felt the little self-control she had slip away.

James stopped before opening the door and turned around, "what?" he said, his voice almost a whisper as if he thought he might have heard wrong.

"Amaryllis what has got into you?" Richard said with a soft voice, looking at his daughter with concerned eyes.

"Apologise to your uncle right now," Lisa said with a stern voice.

"I am not the one that should be apologising," Amaryllis said, mimicking the tone of her mother's harsh voice.

"You know what. That's it. You're grounded. No going out this weekend and tomorrow you come straight home from school," Lisa said. Amaryllis looked at her mother with an expression on her face that said 'how dare you punish me after everything you have done! After cheating on my dad in his own house. After being an unfaithful wife. How dare you punish me because you're afraid I hurt your lover's feelings.'

Amaryllis knew there was no point in arguing with her mother. Whenever she decided something, anything, it was non-negotiable. Even her dad could not argue with her or make her change her mind. Knowing this, Amaryllis stormed out of the dining room, intending to lock herself in her room for the rest of the evening. On her way to the stairs, she noticed that her uncle had already gone. He always ran away when things got complicated or when there was even a bit of confrontation involved. She rolled her eyes, not surprised by his adolescent like behaviour. He loved to do things that he wasn't allowed to do and take risks, but as soon as things got a bit tough, he would run away. Like a rat chased by a cat. In this instance, the rat was her uncle, and she was the cat.

Chapter 3

School Rebel

Slamming the door of her mansion shut, Rose screamed for her mother. The maid came rushing from the kitchen, her white apron stained with green, brown and red colours. ''Miss Rose what's wrong?'' she asked in a panicked voice while fiddling with her hands.

''Where is she?'' Rose screamed, throwing her school bag on the floor, pushing past the maid and going up the stairs. She reached the top of the stairs and barged inside her mother's office. She froze still. The room was packed with people. Some were maids she kind of recognised, but the rest were all men dressed in suits and they all had black briefcases. They wore glasses that sat at the tip of their noses and serious facial expressions were plastered all over their faces. Some of them looked like they were arguing with each other, but Rose couldn't hear a thing. It was as if she was in a silent movie. Then something in her brain clicked.

These people were Lawyers.

She felt her heart skip a beat. These lawyers were probably here to figure out a way to prevent their bankruptcy, Rose thought.

There were so many maids running around the room, carrying trays to serve tea, coffee, biscuits and croissants. Only a few of the lawyers helped themselves to some of the delicious desserts, whilst the rest were too busy to even look up from the papers they were reading.

Her mother must have been calling her name, but Rose couldn't hear anything. She saw her mother look at her and her mouth move in slow motion, but she couldn't make out the words. Then as if someone put sound to the silent movie, all the sound returned to her ears. She heard the arguments the lawyers were having, and she heard them flipping through pages of booklets, furiously crossing things out and calling people on their phones. Correction, they were screaming at them. The sound of the clattering of the plates made when a maid accidentally bumped a plate of biscuits against another snapped Rose's attention to the woman standing right in front of her, staring down at her with a worried expression on her face.

"What's wrong Rose?" her mother asked as she went outside her office and shut the door.

"Are we bankrupt?" she said in such a low voice it was almost a whisper. Rose gulped, afraid of hearing the answer to her question.

Her mother took off her glasses and rubbed her nose, "of course we are not."

"Then why did the cashier tell me my card was stopped?" she asked with tears in her eyes.

Her mother rolled her eyes, "there's a small issue with the bank but it's nothing from our side. There's a technical problem and I will talk with the bank again so they solve it by the end of the day," her mother patted her on the arm gently. Rose threw her arms around her mother and hugged her tightly. She sighed in relief against her chest. Her eyes, however, betrayed her and showed her real emotions. There was a look of uncertainty and something else in them. Fear.

The school bell rang throughout Smith High School. It was a warm and surprisingly sunny Friday morning, and all the students were rushing through the halls, talking about their weekend plans. Except for one sad looking girl with blonde hair. She mooched down the hallway with Rose walking by her side.

"...turns out there was just a technical issue from the bank," Rose finished explaining what had happened yesterday when she had invaded her mother's office to ask if they had gone bankrupt. Not that Amaryllis was paying attention. Rose waved her hand in front of Amaryllis' face, "Amaryllis. Hello, earth to Amaryllis." Finally, Amaryllis snapped her head up to see a disappointed Rose looking down at her.

"Sorry, what did you say?" she asked.

Rose just huffed, "what's wrong with you? I was just telling you that I am not broke," Rose said with a raised eyebrow, her arms crossed in front of her. Amaryllis mumbled a sorry as she and Rose turned left and went into the dining room.

Unlike yesterday, where the centre of the dining room was full of students gathered around and chanting and encouraging a fight, now most students filled the dining tables. Hanging above each table was a huge silver chandelier. Each table seated thirty students and the tables were arranged in rows. Only a few chairs were empty, and the students were devouring their food as if they were prisoners in a concentration camp that had been starved for more than forty-eight hours. While they devoured their food, they were chattering and laughing. Some were throwing food at each other, some were dancing on the tables, and some had their mouths wide open as their friends tried to score food crumbs inside their mouths. If Mrs Smith came in, everybody would receive detention for the rest of the school year. The students, she had said, were supposed to act like respectable young adults from wealthy families and not like children. The only problem was they were still children.

The rest of the students were on the right side of the room where there was a food buffet. They were not presenting themselves any better. They were pushing and hitting each other, wanting to be at the front of the queue. One student got pushed and he sprawled out on the floor on his stomach. Instead of getting up, he lay there and cried like a five-year-old child. The other students snickered at him and called him names. To think that these students were soon going to be adults was worrying.

    The buffet had a section full of desserts. All the desserts anyone craved could be found there. There was a tray full of chocolate cake slices and a tray full of red velvet cakes next to it. Next to the cake trays, was a big tray packed with macarons in many different flavours. There were chocolate, pistachio, strawberry and caramel-filled macaroons. On the other side of the dessert section, there were big square plates filled with middle eastern desserts. One plate served pistachio filled baklava, the next plate served chocolate-filled baklava and the third served big square slices of kunefe filled with cream. Next to the middle eastern heaven, there was a tray overloaded with French toast and small bowls filled to the brim with strawberries, blueberries, raspberries and chocolate chips. Another bowl was filled with cream to serve as a topping for the French toast.

    The students all pushed each other and fought over the French toast, forgetting about the existence of all the other heavenly goods. At the hot food aisle, however, the students were swarming around the roast beef. In three rectangular chafing dishes there laid hot chicken drumsticks covered with a chilli sauce and in the next two chafing dishes were complimentary white rice. The mouth-watering smell of the roast beef could be smelt from a mile away. It was golden brown from all the spices it was seasoned with, and the school made sure to serve a generous amount of roast beef in four rectangular chafing dishes. There were also two round chafing dishes filled with dozens of roasted potatoes, onions, carrots and peppers that went perfectly with the roast beef as well as the gravy served in the three gravy boats. The last aisle was filled with Chinese food. The ramen noodles and egg fried rice served would pair perfectly with the caramelised chicken, Thai sweet chilli chicken curry or the shrimp curry found in separate chafing dishes. Once the students had filled their plates, they would go to the fourth aisle and take tissues, cutlery and salt and pepper if they wanted extra seasonings.

For their drinks, it was less exciting as there were only water and juice machines. This was so students would stay healthy and hydrated. It was against school policy to serve fizzy drinks at the school as it was deemed very unhealthy, which was extremely confusing to all the students because of the number of desserts they served.

Amaryllis and Rose rushed to the meat aisle. A smile spread through Amaryllis' face when she noticed the chicken drumsticks. She took a handful and scooped herself some rice whilst Rose opted for some roast beef and rice with gravy on top. They took small plates and filled them with chocolate macarons. They went to the last aisle and picked up a few napkins and went to the table they usually sat at next to their friends. Their friends included Derek.

And Isabel.

"Oh, there's Derek and Nate...and Natalie is there too," Rose scrunched her face up in disgust as she mentioned Natalie's name.

"Why do you hate her so much?" Amaryllis blurted out before she could stop herself. She seemed to be doing a lot of that lately - speaking without thinking.

Rose arched an eyebrow at her, "I don't hate her," she said, the disgusted expression on her face betraying her. There was no turning back now since the subject had opened, and Amaryllis always wanted to know what Rose had against Natalie. Natalie was always so sweet and fun. Everyone liked her. Even the troublemaker, Isabel.

"No seriously, tell me why. I know you hate her," Amaryllis insisted, making Rose roll her eyes.

"Can we just go and eat. I am starving," Rose said as she turned on her heel and went up to their table. Amaryllis let out an exasperated sigh as she saw her sit next to Derek.

She approached the table and took a seat next to Rose and Natalie, "hey guys," she said.

"Hello bestie," Natalie said as she gave her a side hug. Derek mumbled a hello that was so low Amaryllis wondered if she had hallucinated him greeting her. They spent their lunch eating and chattering, with Amaryllis mostly talking to Rose and Natalie but Rose mostly talking to only Derek. She laughed loudly at anything Derek said. Whenever she laughed Amaryllis snapped her head to look at Rose, but Rose kept her attention on Derek. Derek didn't even spare Rose a glance when he spoke to her. It was as if he didn't even see her. Occasionally he would steal glances at Amaryllis but then Rose would start talking to him about something else. About anything, as long as it got his attention.

Natalie scrunched her face up in disgust as she watched Rose flirt with Derek, "what the hell is wrong with her? She's crossing the red line."

Amaryllis looked at Rose then at Natalie, "she's not flirting with him. She's always liked him as a friend. When we stopped talking, she was so sad because she thought she wouldn't see him as much," Amaryllis rumbled on, trying to convince herself more than she was trying to convince Natalie.

"If you say so, but I didn't even say she was flirting with him so you kind of got to that conclusion by yourself. What does that say?" Natalie said and went back to eating her French toast. She had blueberries, raspberries and dark chocolate drizzled on top of her French toast with cream on the side.

Amaryllis finished eating her plate and turned to Natalie, "do you wanna go shopping?" Natalie had moved her plate with the French toast to the side and was about to start with her second plate of dessert, which was a plate of a small slice of chocolate cake.

"YOU want to SNEAK OUT and skip MATHS?" Natalie said with a shocked face. Then her face broke into a huge smile, "hell yeah! Let's go." Amaryllis smiled at her friend's reaction. Meanwhile, they got up to put their plates away, Rose was too busy flirting with Derek to notice her friend had gone.

As they walked down the hallway Natalie could not stop smiling, "oh my god, I can't believe you are finally turning into a rebel," she squeaked. Amaryllis laughed at her friend, "I am not turning into a rebel. It's just that I am grounded so If I go out after school today my mother will know. Also, we have a substitute teacher. Those teachers don't take attendance and never teach well. I'll just catch up with the work using my textbook at home."

"Ah that's why," Natalie said, still looking at Amaryllis with proud eyes like she had become a rule breaker and wasn't a goody-two-shoes anymore.

After a bit of strolling through the hallway, they arrived at their destination. No, not the shopping centre. The lockers. They emptied their books from their bags and took off their ties so their uniform would look less like a uniform. And it did. Especially with Amaryllis carrying a pink Prada shoulder bag as her school bag and Natalie carrying a Louis Vuitton bag.

Suddenly the school bell rang, indicating the start of the next lesson. Amaryllis and Natalie exchanged looks and then sprinted down the hallway and through the blue school doors. They went through the big golden school gate and hailed a cab, heading for the shopping centre.

After about twenty minutes, they arrived at the shopping centre. Amaryllis paid the driver despite Natalie's protests. First, she attempted to cut Amaryllis' credit card with her scissors, but Amaryllis snatched her card back and managed to throw her card at the driver before Natalie achieved her goal. Afterwards, Natalie attempted to bribe the driver with three hundred pounds if he threw the card out the window and took her card instead, but to Natalie's horror, the driver used Amaryllis''s card.

"Ok but on the way back I'll pay," Natalie said.

"Oh, common it was only twenty pounds," Amaryllis said, waving her hand in the air.

"Even if it was one dollar I do not care." Natalie said as they walked inside the shopping centre.

The shopping centre was huge and the tall building was a purple and pink colour from the exterior. It had seven floors and was called the Grande shopping centre. As they walked further inside, the cool air from the air conditioning hit their skin and cooled their hot bodies that were nearly burned from the blazing summer sun. The first shop they went into was Zara. It was filled with cute mini skirts and had the cutest summer dresses. The first item Amaryllis picked up was a floral pink summer dress. It had a mini length and had spaghetti straps as well as a sweetheart neckline. She showed it to Natalie who immediately dropped the red mini dress she was holding and sprinted to Amaryllis, grabbing the same dress Amaryllis was holding from the clothing rail beside her.

"It's perfection. All a girl could ever wish for," Natalie sang whilst holding the dress in front of her, standing in front of a mirror and inspecting how it would look on her dreamily.

Amaryllis hugged the dress in delight, "it's so pretty but wait until you see the rest of their collection. I saw this blue dress with a square neck as we came in," Amaryllis squealed as she looked around for her prized item.

"There it is," she said excitedly as she rushed to the other side of the room and picked a flowy blue mini dress from the clothing rack. It had white little flowers on it and the bottom part of the dress looked like a skater skirt.

Natalie looked at the dress and squealed, "yay!"

They grabbed a few more things like flats and bags and hats and tops and shorts and bathing suits and then went to the cashier. A moment of Deja vu occurred as Natalie's card got declined by the cashier.

Amaryllis looked at Natalie worriedly, waiting for a meltdown like the one Rose had, but Natalie just laughed. Yes, she laughed. Very loudly in fact. "Oh man I can't believe I have reached my monthly limit already. I mean I have been going shopping every day, but I didn't know it would be finished this soon."

"What's a monthly limit?" Amaryllis asked as she inserted her card to pay for her new wardrobe.

"Oh, basically because I spend so much. Derek and I came up with the idea that I should challenge myself to spend less by putting a limit on how much I can spend every month. After a lot of arguing and fighting, we reached a decision that I should only spend four thousand pounds a month. I knew it would be a challenge, but I had no idea it would be this tough," Natalie said whilst rubbing her chin.

"So just call the bank and increase your limit," Amaryllis suggested as the cashier gave her ten bags.

"The receipt is in one of the bags," the cashier said and smiled. Amaryllis thanked the cashier. She tucked some hair behind her ear and went up to Natalie who was still lost in thought as if she was making a major decision.

"That will take too long, I'll just call dear big brother," Natalie said, and Amaryllis smiled at her friend's easy-going nature.

"Derek... big brotherrr," Natalie almost sang out like a child who wanted a treat.

"Put it on speaker," Amaryllis whispered, motioning with her hands to her phone.

Natalie put it on speaker and Derek's voice rang out, "no, no, no, absolutely not. I know why you are calling, and the answer is no. Do you want it in French, no. Do you want it in Russian, nyet," Derek said. Amaryllis and Natalie giggled and the cashier couldn't help but stifle a laugh.

"Please just this once. I will die if I can't buy these," Natalie said, touching one of the pieces on the counter. When no answer came back Natalie just started whining. "Pleaseeeee. Help your twin out just this once. Pretty pleaseeee with a little cherry on top," Natalie dragged out.

"Okay fine, just stop whining. But you owe me. How much do you want?" Derek said.

There was an explosive silence before Natalie answered him hesitantly, " a thousand pounds." There was another explosive silence as the girls waited for Derek's outburst.

"Where are you? At Louis Vuitton?" he screamed. Amaryllis could not keep it in anymore and just laughed loudly like a dying hyena.

"He thinks you are in Louis Vuitton and only spent a thousand," she continued laughing and bent down clutching her stomach because it started hurting from the pain.

"I am in Zara," Natalie said as she giggled and tried to hush Amaryllis. Then he shut the phone in their faces.

After a few minutes, Natalie looked up at the cashier with a sheepish smile, "Could I please try again? The money has probably gone through to my account." Natalie inserted her card, and the payment was approved.

"Yayyy," she cheered as the cashier packed her treasures and gave her sixteen bags. They walked out of Zara giggling and laughing at Derek and his reactions. Natalie swayed from side to side as she carried her heavy bags and dropped them for the third time. Natalie laughed and picked them up one by one, giving two bags to Amaryllis. "Please help, I can't manage," she giggled.

Chapter 4

Goodbye Ex-Best Friend

The predator stared intently at its prey with its big blue eyes. The prey stopped putting his books into his locker and turned around, staring at the corner of the hall where the predator was hiding. Or attempted to hide. A lock of blonde hair that shone like spun gold gave the predator away. The prey now had a mischievous grin on his face. Pushing his books inside his locker and closing it, he took long strides across the hall and stopped at the corner. The prey had turned into the predator and the predator had turned into the prey. The old predator was now cornered against the wall by the new predator. Derek looked into Amaryllis' eyes; a smirk plastered on his godlike face. How could someone look so perfect? Amaryllis squirmed under his gaze and tried to get away, but he put both his hands on the wall on either side of her head, blocking her exit.

"Have you also reached your monthly limit? Did you also come to ask for money?" he mused.

Amaryllis scoffed, "I don't have a monthly limit."

Derek gave a little laugh that sounded like a beautiful melody, "of course you don't." Derek watched Amaryllis intently, taking in each of her features. Her big blue eyes, her locks of spun gold, her snow-white skin. Amaryllis' breath hitched as Derek started trailing his fingers up and down her bare arms. She was wearing a short-sleeved school shirt today instead of her usual long-sleeved shirt. He continued trailing his fingers up and down her arm until she pushed his hand away and tried to
run. Derek chuckled and grabbed her from the waist and bought her close to his chest. They were so close she could smell his minty breath and feel him exhaling against her bare neck. He put his hand under her chin and drew her face closer to his. Their lips were now a few inches away from each other. Derek leaned in closer, and Amaryllis did too, but just when their lips were about to meet, a scream made them both jump away. They turned their heads to where the sound came from, expecting to see Mrs Smith, but instead, they saw Rose. She looked as if she had seen a ghost.

She looked at them both and pointed her index finger at them, "what are you doing, move away from my best friend." She ran towards Amaryllis and grabbed her by her arm, pulling her towards her. Derek flashed Rose an angry look and Rose almost visibly flinched. It was unusual for Derek to show any negative emotions, he was usually calm and collected and nothing anyone ever did or said could incite any angry or negative emotions from him. But this time was different. For the real predator had stolen his prey. Only God knows how long the real predator had been hiding, waiting and waiting for the right moment to attack. For the right moment to steal his prey. He would now remain hungry and starve without his prey. Maybe even die. Amaryllis kept looking back and forth between Derek and Rose, not knowing what to do.

"Come let's go," Rose dragged Amaryllis by her arm and disappeared into the hall.

After they were a few turns in the hallway away from Derek, Rose stopped and turned around to give her friend a piece of her mind, and also her heart.

"What's wrong with you? Didn't you say you didn't want him?" Rose screamed.

Amaryllis looked taken aback, "wow, why are you screaming at me?" Rose took a deep breath and tried to calm herself down.

"I am not screaming," she said in a much lower voice than before.

"Well, you were screaming," Amaryllis said, her eyes narrowed. Rose gave a little laugh and put her hands on her hips.

"I just don't want to see you get hurt. You saw what happened after your first non-existent date. You were so upset that he stood you up, you didn't come to school for an entire three days and you never skip a day of school," Rose said, trying to sound genuine and concerned but her cold tone and stormy eyes revealed how she felt about Amaryllis.

Amaryllis looked at Rose, her eyes still narrowed. "You know what, drop the act. You don't want me with Derek because you like him. It's obvious. I mean did you even realise I was gone at lunch today? No, you didn't because you were too busy flirting with him," Amaryllis snapped at Rose for the first time. Rose flinched at her friend's tone.

She dropped her sarcastic smile and took a dangerously slow step toward Amaryllis, "so what if I want Derek, what am I not good enough. Am I not blonde enough, not pretty enough like you. What am I not-" her sentence was cut off by an overly excited voice shouting.

"I knew it," Natalie shouted. The blonde ran towards Amaryllis and Rose. Natalie stood there, a wide grin on her face. She looked as if she had been waiting for this moment her entire life. She panted and flipped her silky blonde hair behind her. Rose glared at the beauty with her almost black eyes, eyeing her hair and how it cascaded down like a waterfall on her shoulders. Her eyes then went down to her long legs that made her look like a Victoria's Secret model. Rose, however, was on the opposite end of the beauty scale. Her chubby short legs and big stomach exposed her habit of devouring fast food every day. Natalie must have realised Rose was checking her out because she crossed her arms and made a fake coughing sound, a mischievous smile etched on her face.

"Are you done checking me out yet?" she asked.

Rose rolled her eyes and turned her attention to Amaryllis again, "you think you are perfect and that everybody else is beneath you. News flash, nobody likes you. Even Derek. He left you on your first date because he realised what a spoilt brat you were. And now you are running after him. Can't you take a hint? Just leave him alone. Stop chasing him. Stop bothering him," she said and released a deep breath. Amaryllis stood there in front of this girl that she thought would be her best friend forever. She thought they would travel and experience the world together. She thought they would be by each other's side when they got married and had children. But she was wrong. She had never been so wrong in her entire life.

Natalie's loud laughter broke the deafening silence, "you are so jealous of her. Just because YOU are ugly, and nobody wants YOU. You hate your best friend. Your only best friend. The only person that wants to be around you because she's the only one that can't see through your facade." Natalie held Amaryllis' hand and turned on her heel to leave this theatrical performance. It had continued for far longer than it should have and now it needed to end. Natalie's feet stopped moving when she realised Amaryllis was not moving. Amaryllis let go of Natalie's hand and she took a few steps towards the girl, who up until a few moments ago was her best friend.

"Everyone was right about you," Amaryllis said and turned on her heel. She walked down the hallway with Natalie running to catch up with her fast pace.

"Ok students, find a partner you can complete this activity with," the art teacher announced the next day at school. The whole room erupted in loud chatter and scraping noises were heard as chairs were pulled and moved across the room. The students went from their table to their friend's table and soon everyone was paired up. Natalie whistled and called Amaryllis over, who was busy reading the instructions on the handout.

Meanwhile Rose sat down on her seat looking around for someone that might not mind partnering up with her. No one even spared her a glance. Instant karma. Soon everyone was partnered up except for her. Usually, Amaryllis wouldn't partner up with Natalie or any of her other friends because she knew Rose would be alone. Amaryllis still had her attention focused on the handout. Students whispered and glanced in Rose's direction. Some gave her sympathetic looks. Some giggled. And some were smiling widely from the table Amaryllis sat at. And by some, Natalie was meant.

Natalie had this twinkle in her eye whenever she looked at how Rose was without Amaryllis. Whenever she needed to find a partner in class no one wanted to partner up with her. Whenever she sat at a table during lunch, everybody sitting there would move. She didn't dare to sit at her usual table since she hated almost everyone there and knew there was nobody left that liked her. Therefore at lunch, she sat by herself.

"Well then Miss Rose... ermm..." the teacher said looking around the room to see if there was anyone not partnered up, "why don't you take a picture of yourself and draw yourself," the teacher finished. The whole class evaporated in laughter and Rose just hid her face behind her big frizzy hair. The teacher silenced the class and looked disapprovingly at her students, but the sides of her mouth threatened to twitch up into a smile. Even the teachers did not like Rose. The art teacher started the timer. They each had a chance at drawing a portrait of their partner. Rose snapped a picture of herself on her phone, making everyone giggle silently and then started drawing herself.

Amaryllis held a pencil to draw her best friend whilst Natalie tried to pose dramatically and flip her hair so she would look even more like a Greek goddess. If that was even possible. Amaryllis snickered as she finished drawing her friend's portrait. Natalie looked at Amaryllis wearily and tried to take the portrait from her hands, but Amaryllis just moved it further away from her reach. Natalie complained, got up from her chair and snatched it from Amaryllis' hands. She looked at the portrait with a look of pure disgust, then pure fascination.

"Even with your terrible drawing skills I still don't look as bad as if you would have drawn, yourself for example, or any other average looking person," she said in awe.

"No one can break your self-confidence, but for your information, I am very pretty," Amaryllis said between giggles.

"Yeah, you're ok," Natalie said looking at her from the corners of her eyes. Amaryllis put her hand on her heart, feigning hurt.

A loud sound echoed through the entire school, making all the chatter in the art classroom stop. The teacher stood frozen in her place. After a few seconds, she managed to move her hand and put her pencil down on her desk. She bought her index finger to her lips. She tiptoed to the door and opened it. Peeking her head out a little, she put her hand over her mouth to stop herself from screaming when she heard another loud boom. This time all their doubts were confirmed. It was a gunshot. There was a school shooting.

"Hide under your desks," the teacher whispered as she hid under hers and the students hid under theirs. Some girls and boys were crying whilst others were shushing them angrily. Footsteps could be heard down the hallway, and they were getting louder and louder. Suddenly the footsteps stopped, and the door was thrown open, causing a girl to scream.

"Shshshshsh," her classmates shushed her.

"What are you guys doing?" a familiar voice said. Everyone looked up. There, stood a clueless Nate.

"Get under your table. There's a school shooting," the teacher whispered harshly. Nate gave his teacher a big goofy smile and then his eyes widened as he registered what the teacher had said to him. He closed the door gently and stomped to his desk, causing the students to angrily shush him. He put his chubby frame under the table and bent down on his hands and knees, his butt sticking out like he was a cat getting ready to pounce on a mouse. Amaryllis and Natalie couldn't help but snicker but quieted down when another pair of footsteps could be heard approaching their classroom. Fingers crossed it was just another student. The door was thrown open with such a force, it hit the wall with a loud slam and the walls shook. The person stepped into the classroom and slammed the door shut. When no shots were fired Amaryllis looked through the tiny crack in her desk but covered her mouth in shock after seeing a hooded figure. He was tall and fat. He was wearing an all-black outfit and only his eyes could be seen. He had a big gun in his left hand whilst his right hand rested on his hip. His lifeless eyes met Amaryllis' blue ones for a second and he stomped forward to her desk. He reached down and grabbed her from her hair.

"Ahhh," she screamed as he yanked her hair.

"Shut up you spoilt bitch. I don't want to hear a word coming out of your mouth," he hissed in her ear.

"Well that's rud-," Natalie poked her head from under her table and started lecturing away, but stopped when she realised whom she was lecturing. She hid under her desk again and pretended as if she did not exist.

Amaryllis just shook her head at her friend. She knew nothing could keep her quiet. But now? Now she could've kept quiet. At least for her sake, since he was planning on killing her first. But maybe that was better. If he killed her first, then she wouldn't have to wait to be killed.

"You there, blondie, get out of there before I drag you out as I did with your friend," the shooter demanded with his clumsy mouth. For the first time in all her seventeen years of existence, Natalie was silent. She stayed under her desk, not daring to even breathe.

"Get out I said," he roared like the beast he was. Or maybe a beast would've been more merciful. He let go of Amaryllis' hair, making her fall to the ground and grunt in pain as she clutched her ankle. He yanked Natalie from her hair whilst she kicked and screamed until he put his gun to her head.

"Well, that's rude. First, you drag me from my beautiful silky hair, which by the way I spend hours on every morning and now you are just pulling it, ahhh," she said and screamed the last few words angrily as he pulled her hair harder and harder with every word that left her mouth.

"Everyone get up from under your desks otherwise I will kill every single one of you," he said. Everyone, including the teacher, shuffled out from under their desks. Their legs shook as they walked, and their bodies trembled.

"Now stand against the wall, your back facing me," he said, pointing with his gun at the wall. With his gun, he motioned for Amaryllis to go to the wall too. She looked back at Natalie who had tears brimming her eyelashes and limped to the wall. He scrutinised Natalie with his dark eyes and finally released his hold on her hair. He pointed to the wall. She didn't need to be told twice as she sprinted to the wall and stood beside Amaryllis. All the students were in shock, school shootings sometimes happened in the United States, but never in England. What was even more shocking was that it happened in this private school. This school was expected to have more security in place than any other normal school. It was expected to prevent any dangerous incidents from occurring and to protect its students from any lurking dangers. At least that's what Mrs Smith had promised the parents of the students before their children started attending this school. She had promised them that there were various safety measures in place and that the police themselves made the protection of this school a priority. How deceitful. They fooled the students and parents with the many luxuries they provided for the students like the trips to Europe and stays in expensive five-star hotels, where all the costs were covered by the school. This made them think the same effort was being directed towards their safety. Such a deceiving yet beautiful lie. Now they would die. Just because the school did not care for the safety of its students and did not have any safety measures in place. Or so they thought.

"So, who should I kill first?" the monster roared once again.

"How about you," he started pulling the trigger and aimed his gun at…

Chapter 5

The Upper Class Party

...Nate. The chubby boy hid his face with his hands whilst his body trembled.

"Move your hands away from your face, you pathetic boy," the shooter hissed whilst pulling the trigger further, but Nate just shook his head vigorously.

Amaryllis saw Nate's fate and decided to bravely confront the attacker, "leave him alone." The art teacher and everyone in the classroom looked at her as if she had lost her mind. It was not like the shooter would listen to her and stop killing poor Nate. But he did stop. The shooter stopped pulling the trigger. Instead, he pointed his gun at Amaryllis. Everyone in the classroom gasped, apart from Nate who started wailing and stomping his feet on the ground like a three-year-old boy who wanted dessert when his mother had decided he had already had too much. The shooter looked between Amaryllis and Nate, his eyes turning from lifeless to rageful.

"Is this a game? Are you two conspiring against me?" the shooter said, pointing his gun at Nate and then at one random student after another. Amaryllis had a second to sigh in relief before the gun was pointed at her again. "You can't win. I will kill all of you. Rich people can't win all the time. It's just not fair," the shooter screeched. He raised his arm and fired two shots at the ceiling, making a few girls scream in their high-pitched annoying voices. Some students crouched down to the ground and some covered their ears.

Pointing his gun at Amaryllis again, her eyes stared into his lifeless ones. They looked like all the sadness and despair of the world existed in them. They were like a lifeless grave. Cold. Lonely. Dead. Amaryllis couldn't imagine what the shooter must have gone through in his life to make him want to kill innocent students. What could have been so horrible that he had taken the liberty upon himself to trespass into a random private school and kill its students? She took a second look into those almost pitch-black eyes. They looked familiar. They certainly didn't belong to someone she was very close to. However, she had a feeling she had seen them before. More than once. She searched her memory but came up blank.

She decided she would use the remainder of her time left to think about her family. She thought about her mother, her father and even her uncle and how she wouldn't get a chance to say goodbye. Her father had just come back from his trip, and she hadn't had a chance to spend any time with him. She also thought about her mother. Although they had their differences, she still loved her mother. She would now die and the last thing that she would remember was her mother being unfaithful. She also still loved her uncle despite everything and it pained her that the last memory of him would be the same as that of her mother. Amaryllis was brought back to reality as the shooter tapped his foot impatiently against the floor. Just as he was about to pull the trigger, the door was flung open. Everyone flinched.

"Put your gun down, POLICE!" a policeman shouted aiming his gun at the shooter. He cautiously made his way towards the shooter, four policemen following behind him. They surrounded the shooter whilst more police swarmed in through the door.

"Put your gun down and put your hands up where I can see them," a policewoman called out. Whether the shooter was deaf or stupid was not clear because he did not put his gun down. His fingers were still pulling the trigger, and the gun was still aimed at poor Amaryllis. Natalie's cheeks were coated with dried tears as she looked at her best friend's drained face. She looked like she was already dead, her face was as pale as death and her eyes had lost the sparkle they always had. Rose stole a peek at her ex-best friend and then looked away as if she had not looked at all.

"If you don't put your gun down, we will shoot you," the policewoman called out again, after the shooter did not comply with her first orders. That's when the shooter pulled the trigger. It was as if everything was in slow motion. A shot left the gun and travelled in the direction of Amaryllis' head but before it had the chance to pierce through her skin, Natalie had already pushed Amaryllis and herself to the floor. The shot hit the wall and within seconds a policeman had already shot the shooter in the back. Twice. The first time he was shot, he did not let go of his gun and still attempted to fire another shot at Amaryllis. After the second shot, the gun dropped from his hand. Three policemen tackled him to the ground whilst a policewoman grabbed his gun.

Carried out in a stretcher, with both his hands cuffed, the shooter was carried to the ambulance. All the students and the teachers watched as they unmasked the shooter and put their PE teacher inside the ambulance car. Mr Andrews was always kind, supportive and was voted best teacher in their year several times in the past six months. The students watched with shocked expressions as their beloved teacher was driven away in the ambulance with several police cars travelling close behind. Amaryllis and Natalie stood there, anger in their usually happy eyes. How could he do this? How could he try to kill Amaryllis and Natalie? Just a few days ago he said they were his favourite students. Maybe they were his favourite to kill. The school bell rang, indicating the end of the day. Thank the blue heavens. They all shuffled inside, going into their classrooms and picking up their bags and books. It was awfully quiet, unlike the usual Fridays where students ran down the hallways, impatient to get out of school and go out with their friends. They would go to a shopping mall, a party or maybe even arrange an overnight trip to Paris. Today they left the school building with each student checking their surroundings for anything or anyone that might be a threat and then their chauffeurs drove them straight home.

Tension filled the air as classical music was being played by the orchestra Lisa had hired and everyone present at the party was wearing white. All the students from the school and their parents were invited, as well as others from the upper class. Though, less than half of the students and their parents showed up. Those were the sensible ones that realised that they needed to deal with the trauma of what had happened and not party their way through it.

Amaryllis stood in front of the large pool in her garden looking at her reflection in the water. She was wearing a white midi dress with a leg slit and straps that were embellished in yellow gems. Her white dress had a few streaks of yellow, making her stand out from all the other strangers that wore fully white. Her tired eyes scanned around the garden of her home, but her eyes only recognised a few students that she had maths lessons with. She hoped none of them would try and speak with her because speaking to anyone right now was the last thing she wanted to do. She didn't want to pour her heart out to anyone nor did she want to pretend she was fine.

Someone tapped her shoulder from behind and she spun around to find the person she least wanted to see standing there. Rose smiled and it looked like a genuine smile, but Amaryllis knew otherwise. Amaryllis sighed tiredly, an unreadable expression on her face. Rose raised an eyebrow as if waiting for Amaryllis to say something.

"Aren't you going to say hello to your best friend?" Rose asked, her eyebrow still raised; a fake smile mastered on her lips once again.

"Are you serious? Best friend?" Amaryllis scoffed, spun around and started walking away. Rushing up to her, Rose cut in front of her, a wicked grin now replaced the sweet smile.

"Move. Away. From. Me," Amaryllis said through gritted teeth, emphasising every word.

"Oh common. Are we going to stop talking to each other after one fight? We have been friends since reception," Rose said, trying to reach for Amaryllis' hand, but she moved it out of her reach. Rose's wicked grin was quickly replaced with an angry scowl.

She opened her mouth but closed it when someone came and stood next to Amaryllis. Amaryllis felt herself unconsciously leaning into the warmth that suddenly appeared next to her. Her saviour made Rose squirm under his intense gaze and she stomped away, but not before casting one last dirty look at Amaryllis.

    Her saviour wore a black suit with a white shirt, the first few buttons undone. He had his blazer open and a red bow was stuffed in his pocket. Derek was not one to follow rules, especially rules about attire. He looked intently into Amaryllis' eyes, worry filling his usually emotionless eyes. He tucked a strand of blonde hair behind her left ear, and they stayed like that staring into each other's eyes. Talking to each other with their eyes, listening to each other's troubles through their eyes. For a moment they were lost in their world, but a loud voice brought them back to reality.

    "Welcome everyone," Lisa's voice boomed excitedly as if her daughter wasn't about to be killed a few days ago. She stood behind a high round table in the middle of the garden and had a microphone in her hand. All the guests stood behind their assigned table and watched as Lisa made her toast. "We are celebrating our children's safe return home today," Lisa continued whilst looking at her guests, not sparing her daughter a glance. She finished her endearing speech and raised her wine glass to toast for their children's safe return home. Amaryllis rolled her eyes at her mother's cry for attention. Even at a time like this, she wanted to be the centre of attention. She even wore a red dress when she had specifically stated that the dress code was white in the invites to the party. Not to mention the number of times she flipped her freshly styled hair.

    Amaryllis' eyes shifted from her mother to her uncle, who was busy laughing and talking with a raven-haired beauty. She noticed her mother scrutinize her uncle from the corner of her eyes, but that only lasted a few seconds as her focus went back to her guests. For a split second, you could see her fake smile fall slightly as she watched her lover flirt with another woman, but she mastered her fake smile and continued with her speech. Wearing a fake smile was a skill she had mastered. It was her mask. With her mask on, nobody could hurt her. Whatever she was going through, people would think she was strong as they would not be able to see her real emotions. A grin formed on Amaryllis' face that did not reach her eyes. She took a sip of her wine, letting it do its job of calming down her nerves.

If Derek hadn't coughed, she would have forgotten he was standing beside her. She felt him pull her arm gently and lead her out of the crowded garden party. She walked with him, past the rose bushes, and past a couple of trees that stood tall and strong despite the storms England had recently had. Their feet stopped moving when they reached two trees that were bent down towards each other, making an almost heart shape. They stood behind the heart, their eyes locking.

"I.. erm," Derek struggled to say. He had his head down, meanwhile, Amaryllis was waiting patiently for what he was going to say. That was the least she could do after ignoring him for weeks after he didn't show up for her date. He summoned his courage and looked up at her. The next three words that left his mouth left Amaryllis both miserable and ecstatic at the same time. Those next three words reminded her of her mother's infidelity. It reminded her of the uncle she used to go on adventures with. The only person that could cheer her up after she got a bad grade or one of her mother's lectures, but also the one that was cheating with her mother.

"I missed you," he said and her face broke into a genuine smile for the first time in a few days.

"I know you are angry at me because I didn't show up that day but if you just let me ex-," she cut him off by placing a finger on his lips.

"I don't care. That's in the past," she said. "I missed you too." Her cheeks were now tinted with a rosy colour as she fiddled with the side of her dress. Derek took her hand in his. He leaned in for a kiss and so did she. As their lips met for a moment, a loud noise in the sky startled them, making them pull away. They looked up at the sky and saw the beautiful fireworks. Some were pink, some were blue. Some were red, some were purple and the rest were many different colours. Nearly all the colours of the rainbow were there. They laughed and leaned in again to finish their kiss as more fireworks exploded in the sky. What a perfect movie moment.

They were so busy with each other that they didn't notice someone was watching them. She watched them like a predator watches its prey before it pounces and kills it. There, hiding behind one of the trees was Rose. She stared at them as they kissed and laughed happily, a look of disdain on her ugly face. Moving her leg forward, she accidentally stepped on a tree branch, breaking it in half. Amaryllis and Derek twirled their heads around in the direction of the noise, but Rose quickly hid behind the tree. They went back to kissing each other when they didn't see anyone. Rose peeked her head out and shot Amaryllis one last hateful look before she turned around and walked to the garden party. On her way back to her table she bumped her shoulder past Natalie, "watch it," she screeched. Natalie looked back at her and rolled her eyes.

"Crazy bitch," She whispered and sipped her wine.

Everyone was seated at the biggest table ever made in history. It stretched from one end of the garden, all the way from the heart tree until the white fence on the other side of the garden. About two hundred guests sat at the table. It was draped in a white cloth, with small vases that had a pink peony in them placed throughout the table. Candles placed in silver candlesticks were also placed throughout the table. There were different varieties, flavours and colours of food served. There were trays of steak and roasted potatoes and veggies. There were also trays of sushi, smoked salmon, rice and bowls of asparagus and colourful side salads.

Everyone was eating whilst they conversed and laughed loudly. It didn't take long for Natalie to get over the shocking event as she chattered away with Isabel and devoured her sushi.

Everyone seemed to be in their own world and did not take notice of Amaryllis and Derek secretly and silently shooting each other romantic glances and smiling at one another every now and then. Amaryllis reached her hand down to her chair and interlocked her fingers with Derek's. Derek did the same and smiled at her. However, there was one other person that was silent. Rose. She was sitting opposite Derek and Amaryllis and was watching them like a hawk. Rose took a big bite of her steak and chewed it aggressively as she watched the two lovebirds live in a world of their own. Rose was also in a world of her own.

She was so busy in her own world that she did not notice Natalie watching her. With every single opportunity she got, when she was not talking with Isabel or throwing a joke here and there to random strangers that sat beside her, she would look at Rose. Then she would look at where Rose was looking which would lead her to her brother and Amaryllis. She didn't understand why Rose was so angry when she watched them.

There was nothing between Amaryllis and Derek anymore. They were just sitting next to each other. Thinking again, she concluded that to a maniac that would be the same thing. Natalie glared at Rose, hoping that she would feel her glare so she could turn around and she could give her a piece of her mind. She couldn't exactly shout across a couple of seats because that would result in a scandal. Gossip spread fast in the upper class. Especially through social media apps like Instagram. Leave them alone, she wanted to say. You've already hurt Amaryllis. My brother would never look at you, she also wanted to say, a bit more aggressively. And then she would go back to eating her food in peace. Or maybe she would not. Maybe she would take a swing with her fist at Rose's ugly face.

  Once everyone had finished their dinner, servants came in, men who wore white trousers and shirts with a white bow, and women who wore mini white dresses with a tiny apron around their waist. They picked up all the plates and trays and then bought in the bowls and trays of fruit. There were trays of pineapples cut up into heart shapes. There were bowls of raspberries, strawberries and blueberries. There were trays of watermelon cubes, green grapes and kiwis and jugs of orange juice. Everybody helped themselves and filled their plates up with all kinds of different fruits that were there as if they didn't just eat a whole meal.

  "Make sure you leave room for dessert," Lisa said whilst laughing and everybody joined in with the unnecessary laughter. Amaryllis looked at her uncle who was still flirting with his new target. The raven heard beauty sat next to James and opposite his lover. He kept telling her his usual memorised jokes that he told all the women he pursued. She seemed to think the jokes were hilarious and laughed louder and louder with every joke. James touched her arm every now and then, making Lisa's hand clench around the fork she was eating with. Amaryllis watched as her father looked at his wife worriedly.

"Honey what's wrong?" he asked her.

"Nothing," she responded, unclenching her hand. She reached for her glass of wine and drank her jealousy away. James watched Lisa's reaction, an evil twinkle in his eyes, the corners of his mouth nearly tugging up to form a smile. She gave him the evil eye as she continued gulping down her pinot noir.

Amaryllis bought her attention back to her plate full of blueberries and raspberries, unable to watch this ridiculous drama any longer. She poked around with her food, not feeling like eating any longer. Derek's eyes lit up with concern as he watched Amaryllis play with her food. She loved raspberries and always devoured them as soon as she got hold of them. She smiled reassuringly at Derek and forced some raspberries down her throat to convince him she was fine. Everybody that could still bring themselves to eat, which was nearly everyone, ate their troubles away whilst the orchestra was still playing the same boring classical tune it was playing at the start of the party.

Chapter 6

Uncle and Niece

"Attention everyone. I have a big announcement to make," Rose called out using a loudspeaker. She was standing in the middle of the dining room, with a big book in one hand and a loudspeaker in the other. Students stopped eating and jerked their heads in the direction of the person interrupting their lunchtime.

Amaryllis, Derek and Natalie had just walked in and noticed a crowd forming around Rose. She was standing there, her uniform messy as always with one of her knee-high socks above her knee and the other fallen to her ankle. Her shirt was not tucked in, and it hung loosely over her short navy skirt. Her frizzy hair added to her messy look with half of it falling over her left eye and the rest sticking out in all different directions, making her look like she was electrocuted.

    Amaryllis, Derek and Natalie made their way to the food aisle, going past Rose. Today's lunch was all vegetarian. One aisle served vegetable spring rolls, egg fried rice, vegetarian sushi and some cabbage salad. The other aisle that they were in served an Indian vegetable curry dish with white rice and some side salad. Amaryllis picked up the serving spoon and was about to take some rice when Rose's next sentence made her hand stop mid-air.

    "Amaryllis has been obsessed with Derek for years. She's so obsessed with him that she's made this scrapbook full of pictures of both of them together," Rose said, opening the scrapbook full of pictures of Derek and Amaryllis. More students left their tables and hurried towards Rose, wanting to see and hear the latest gossip. Rose flipped the page, revealing a picture of Amaryllis and Derek. They were two separate pictures that had been cut and put together. One could tell just by looking at the background of the picture since each half had a different background. The crowd erupted in laughter when they saw that Amaryllis had put a veil on her head, showing she was fantasising about marrying Derek. There was also another picture of Derek and Amaryllis from year ten, where she had attached a flower sticker on Derek's hand, making it look like he had bought her flowers. The third picture on that page was a picture of Amaryllis and Derek and a little baby that looked like both of them. Rose was explaining how Amaryllis had gone on an app and used a photo of her and a photo of Derek to predict what their future children would look like. Amaryllis put her head down as Derek looked at her, an amused expression on his face. Judging by the tears forming in her eyes,

Amaryllis didn't think this was funny at all. Rose didn't seem satisfied enough with her state and went on.

"And the biggest shock is that she has been doing this for years, ever since she was fifteen. How do I know this you may ask? I know this because I used to make these pictures with her. I used to be her best friend but after realising what a crazy person she is, I am no longer her friend," Rose said with a loud snicker. The dining room boomed with laughter as some were pointing at Amaryllis and directing insults at her, calling her things like 'crazy,' and 'love lunatic.' This made Derek's hands form into fists and his eyes harden. He bought his hand up and brushed Amaryllis' hair away from her face. His eyes immediately softened when he noticed her tears. He bought her into his chest and put his arm around her waist, hugging her from the side. Natalie saw this and immediately took out her camera that she had somehow managed to fit in the pocket of her skirt and snapped a picture of the two.

"To add to your amazing scrapbook," she said more to herself than her friend and grinned. Derek stared at his sister as if she was insane. He mouthed something to her, and she turned to silence Rose, but someone beat her to it.

"Enough already. Is this how you treat your friends? You go and tell all their secrets to everyone. No wonder no one wants to be your friend," A voice called out from the other side of the room. The mystery person approached Rose, pushing through the crowds. Or, did the crowds move to make way for her? Finally getting through to where Rose was, stood no one other than Isabel. Yes, that Isabel. The one that had slut shamed Amaryllis in front of her friends. She stood tall and confident as she always did.

The crowds started murmuring and whispering, albeit confused by the sudden turn of events.

A few days ago, Isabel had been the one to shame Amaryllis and insult her and Rose was cheering Amaryllis on when she attacked Isabel. After the detention Amaryllis, her friends and Isabel received, the whole school found out what had happened with no effort at all. Amaryllis looked at Isabel with surprise in her eyes, but Isabel kept her attention on Rose.

"Everyone go and finish your lunch, there's nothing to see here," Natalie said, shooing the crowd away to the left side of the room where the dining tables were. Derek was still there, comforting Amaryllis and running his hands down her hair. It was such a simple gesture yet when he did it, he could feel her relax. Rose noticed what Derek was doing and turned the scrapbook page to the last page. Before she could open her mouth, Natalie snatched the book from her hand. Rose pounded her feet on the ground and reached her hand for the book, but Natalie pushed her away. Rose stumbled and nearly fell but regained her balance.

"And you, why don't you go and brush your hair or style it with some gel, so you look less like a witch and more like a girl. I can give you some recommendations if you want," Natalie said whilst playing with her silky hair. Rose looked at her hair and touched the frizzy mess. She looked at Natalie's hair with an envious look in her eyes and grabbed Natalie by her locks, prompting a growl from Derek and a shriek from Natalie.

"Let go of my sister," he said menacingly and if looks could kill Rose would have already been a thousand feet under the ground. Rose shifted under Derek's gaze and let go of Natalie's hair. Isabel had already gone to the food aisle when the crowd was gone. She watched with interest as they fought whilst she began to scoop herself some lunch. Natalie rushed towards Amaryllis and Derek, and they rushed out of the dining room and into one of the empty classrooms. They sat down on the chairs and Derek wiped some of the tears that managed to escape from his girlfriend's eyes. She sniffed and pushed her hair out of her face, looking up at Derek.

"You probably think I am crazy now, don't you?" she asked.

He looked at her with half-confused eyes half-amused ones, "why would I think that. We have always liked each other. There's nothing 'crazy' about you fantasising about me, especially since we are dating now," he said, doing the bunny ears sign around the word crazy.

"I can't believe you two didn't tell me you were together! Maybe I should thank that span of Satan. If it wasn't for what she did I probably would have never found out," Natalie said, huffing and turning her head away from them.

"We just wanted to take it slow, without any pressure or expectations from anyone," Amaryllis said, grabbing some concealer from her blazer pocket to hide the redness around her eyes.

"If we told you the whole of England would know," Derek said raising an eyebrow at his sister.

"Ah well, now everybody knows," Natalie said, taking her phone out of her pocket and opening her Instagram. Amaryllis looked at Natalie's skirt pocket as if it was a magical object. Natalie seemed to be able to fit everything in there.

Natalie showed them a snapshot of them talking to each other just a second ago with the caption, 'it's official they are dating.' Derek tried to steal the phone from Natalie's hand, but she just gave it to him. Derek raised a confused eyebrow. Natalie grinned and shrugged. He went to delete the post but then saw the number of people that had already seen the story. Two-thousand people had viewed it already. Derek gave her back her phone whilst Amaryllis was sitting in her chair, still applying her concealer. She knew that if Natalie posted something on her story, then everyone would have seen it, so it would be useless to delete it. Amaryllis knew he had already accepted reality. Out of the blue, Derek grabbed Natalie's phone making Natalie yell in protest. He opened her Instagram and went to her photos and scrolled through them.

"Why are most of your photos of you in a bikini? Delete them," he ordered.

Natalie's eyes gleamed with confidence and she took her phone back, "never and I can post whatever I want." Derek looked at his sister with a hurt look as if she had done something to him, but this only made Natalie giggle.

Amaryllis said her goodbyes to Natalie and sneaked a kiss on Derek's cheek before any of the teachers could see them. He tried to sneak a kiss on her lips, but Amaryllis ducked down. She skipped to her car and Derek chuckled and went to his car where Natalie stood watching the two in awe, her camera in her hand. Legend says she had already made an entire album for them.

Amaryllis sat in her car and whilst she was pulling her seat belt, her phone buzzed. Excited, she reached for her phone quickly thinking it was her lover, but she was wrong. It was not her lover but the monster, the monster that had started tearing her family apart. She ignored the texts and locked her phone. She looked out of the window, trying to ignore the constant buzzing her phone was making, but it kept buzzing and buzzing. She could no longer ignore it. She opened her text messages and started reading through the dozens of texts her uncle had sent her. He asked her if she wanted to go skydiving.

She sighed, remembering how many times she had begged him to take her and now that she was old enough, she didn't want to go with him. She did not want to go anywhere with him or even be in the same room as him.

The last few text messages read, "why are you ignoring me? Are you upset with me? You haven't spoken to me in over a week." Before she knew it the driver had pulled into her driveway and had opened the car door for her. She stepped out of her car and shoved her phone into her bag. She stopped dead in her tracks when she saw her uncle standing in front of her. His blue eyes stared intently into hers. They were not the usual happy excited eyes she was used to. They were sad, worried and full of despair. For a second, she wondered if she had been the cause of all that sadness or maybe her mother had finally left him. Since everything in her life was going downhill, she decided to go with option number one. She walked past her uncle who walked after her at the same fast pace she walked in.

"Welcome-," the maid greeted her, but Amaryllis hurried past her and slammed the door shut in her uncle's face. She could hear him swear as he knocked and waited for the maid to open the door for him.

Amaryllis smiled to herself and went into the living room. The living room had a large pink couch with small square pillows that had satin pillowcases. There were two small sofas identical to the big one on the left and right side of the room.

Next to the glamorous sofa, there was a small white rectangular table full of fashion magazines and business magazines. Lisa had passed on her love of fashion to her daughter and for that reason, fashion magazines were found scattered around the house everywhere. Under the rectangular table, was a small pink and white Persian carpet. Opposite the big sofa, there was a huge tv screen that was nearly as big as a cinema screen. Lastly, in each corner of the room, there was a huge plant.

"Are you kidding me. What's wrong with you?" her uncle shouted as he strode into the living room. He looked furious, with his messy blonde hair all over his face and his face red with rage. He gritted his teeth, taking deep breaths to calm himself down. Amaryllis scrunched her face up in disgust, watching him trying to calm himself down. Pathetic. She watched as his chest heaved up and down, clearly his attempt at calming himself failed.

"What have I done to upset you? Don't say it's nothing because you've never acted like this before. I mean sure you get your mood swing especially when you have your monthly visit to the red world, but you've never behaved like this," he finished, panting. A moment passed as Amaryllis looked him up and down as if she was looking and checking the quality of meat before buying. She scrunched up her face in disappointment, not satisfied with the quality of the meat and decided to say just that to her uncle's face.

"You are having an affair with my mother, and I know all about it," she said. She threw herself down on the pink sofa, putting her hand on the sofa arm and sunk deeper into the warmth of the sofa, a smile forming on her face as she watched her uncle's reaction. She watched as his face grew pale and all the colour drained from it. Then and there she decided she had had enough of being mistreated, lied to and manipulated. Not Rose, not her uncle and not even her mother were going to mistreat her anymore. From now on she was going to face her bullies. She was going to stand up for herself and defend herself.

"Sweetheart you are confused. Your mother is like a sister to me," he said, changing his tone from enraged to sweet. Amaryllis noticed this was a way of manipulation, to act sweet and nice so the other person would believe you. She chuckled and stood up from the couch. She had this mischievous twinkle in her eyes, one which you would not usually see in her eyes but Derek's or Natalie's.

She took a few steps towards her uncle, "You should just not say anything because that makes this whole thing a lot more disgusting."

"You are just confused. You have been watching too many of those Turkish dramas of yours and those Spanish telenovelas," he said, turning around and walking away.

"I heard you two kissing in the guest room that day and I heard you confess how much you missed her," she said, making him stop dead in his tracks.

He spun around faster than the wind and took fast angry steps towards her. He grabbed her by the arms, "I've had enough of you, you little brat." Amaryllis stared right into his eyes. She wasn't scared of him. The only emotion she felt right now was hate. She pushed him away, making him release his hold on her. Her uncle stepped back, a look of instant regret washed over his face, as if he just realised what he had done. He fiddled with his hands as if not knowing what to do with them, but then settled and put them by his sides.

"Everything is not how it seems," her uncle said. Amaryllis almost laughed. She laughed. Hard. She only stopped laughing when she heard her dad's voice coming from the hallway. A head full of brown hair popped through the living room door. Her dad smiled at her and put down the box of chocolate macaroons he got for his daughter every Monday from La Rose. His eyes darted between his brother and his daughter, no doubt noticing the tension in the room.

"Did something happen?" He asked.

"No," they said in unison before cracking a smile at Richard. Richard hugged his daughter and went upstairs to change his clothes whilst Amaryllis waited for him to be out of sight so that she could resume her bickering. Instead, James decided to leave the living room.

Amaryllis had always loved that she looked so much like her uncle. She shared his blue eyes and blonde hair. She looked more like him than she looked like her parents. Her mother had blonde hair but had brown eyes just like her dad. Now she hated the resemblance. She wished she had her dad's brown hair and brown eyes. Now every time she would look in the mirror, she would see that lying backstabbing son of a bitch.

"We aren't finished here. We are still going to talk about this, just not now," he said as he exited the living room quickly.

"Oh, but I am finished. There's nothing more we need to talk about," she called after him. He was trying to run away from her. She wasn't surprised since he was known to run away any time things got hard or he wanted to avoid any confrontations. One time he cheated on his then fiancé. Her name was Rebecca. As soon as he found out she knew about his affair, he booked a flight to Hawaii and only returned after she stopped coming to Amaryllis' house to ask about his whereabouts. Amaryllis had then texted him to tell him it was safe to come home. How she wished she had let Rebecca have him. Maybe she would have taught him a lesson or two about being honest and loyal. And how to not stab people in the back.

She watched as he went up the stairs, not bothering to shout anything back, most likely because there was nothing else he could say. She had caught him red-handed and he could deny his sins all day and night, for the rest of his life, but he could never convince her of his innocence. She didn't even need to put him on trial. To her he was guilty and no excuse in the world could make him innocent. What was he going to say, your mother forced me to kiss her?

She relaxed on the couch, putting her head back on the soft material and she stretched her arms. After the day she had, she would need a long bath. Preferably with lavender bath bombs and a glass of white wine. Maybe some grapes in a bowl too.

Chapter 7

Steak the French Way

    Derek looked at pictures of the Lamborghini Aventador SVJ. He swiped through the pictures on his laptop and smirked mischievously. That was the car his friend would soon owe him. His eyes were set on the green Lamborghini. He had thought about getting the pink Lamborghini but thought it looked too girly. His phone buzzed and a text message from Amaryllis appeared. Derek looked over at the screen and tapped his fingers on his desk. He turned his phone over so it was facing downwards.

    For just a split second, a look of regret might have been spotted on his face, but it disappeared as quickly as it had appeared. He returned his attention to his laptop screen and scrolled down to look at the details and the price of his prize. The maximum speed it reached was around 300km/h and Nicholas would soon have to spend thousands on his dream car. His phone started ringing, snapping Derek out of his dream world.

Derek sighed deeply but picked his phone up. When he saw Nicholas' written on the screen he smiled and accepted the call excitedly.

"You should kiss your Lamborghini goodbye. Time is nearly up," Nicholas laughed through the other end of the phone.

"Get your money ready because you'll soon be buying me that car," Derek said smugly. All Derek could think about right now was that car. How he would fly like the wind when he drove it and how everyone would watch him with jealousy and envy and wish they were him. He thought about how all the girls would swoon over him and throw themselves at him just to ride in his car. Not that they didn't already swoon over him.

Despite all the excitement that came with daydreaming about the car, Derek's thoughts seemed to manage to drift elsewhere. He would not admit that he sometimes thought about Amaryllis and how heartbroken she would be when she found out about everything. How sadness would fill her beautiful sky-blue eyes. How she might not even spare a hello to him again.

Shaking those thoughts out of his head and that guilty feeling out of his heart, he brought his attention and his thoughts back to his Lamborghini. At the end of the day, the Lamborghini would stay with him for years, but Amaryllis might dump him over any small misunderstanding. That's what happened with his first girlfriend. She left him because he liked another girl's picture on Instagram. That's how girls were. They were emotional and sensitive and got upset over anything.

"Derek, dinner is ready," his mother called from downstairs. Derek said goodbye to his friend and took one last look at his dream car before he closed the laptop screen.

Amaryllis stared at her plate full of broccoli, carrots and plain white rice. She hated broccoli and her mother knew that. Nevertheless, that did not stop her from serving it today for dinner. The chef had been away for today and so her mother had to put her creativity to the test. There would be no need to ask for a rating from everyone at the table as zero would be an obvious score from anyone. The broccoli and carrots were raw. She had not even bothered to cook them. The carrots still had some outer skin on them, and the rice was plain and unseasoned.

Amaryllis picked up her fork and looked at her mother who was smiling proudly as she watched everyone eat. Amaryllis peered at her dad who gave her a smile of encouragement and motioned with his fork for her to eat. She took a bite of her carrot and grinned fakely at her mother as she watched everyone taste her food.

Her uncle was eating in silence, not daring to look up at his niece, who a few hours ago, had thrown the fact that she knew about his affair so blatantly in his face.

"Amaryllis, James told me he was going to take you skydiving, are you excited about that sweetheart?" Richard asked, beaming. At the mention of this, James tensed in his seat. Amaryllis stopped eating her rice and looked up at her father with a mouth full of carrots. She chewed them quickly and cleared her throat when she finished her bite.

Wiping the side of her mouth that was smudged with a non-existing sauce she said, "oh no we aren't going anymore." Her uncle stopped eating and gave her an aggravated look. She silently mimicked his action before smiling sweetly at her dad.

Her father's eyes drifted between her and her uncle. He had noticed their heated exchange and was very confused. First, he sensed the tension between them in the afternoon and now Amaryllis was making excuses not to go skydiving, which she had been dreaming about going for years.

"I am afraid I've developed a terrible fear of heights," she said whilst looking upset as if she was missing out on their trip. Thankfully, her mother kept eating and cringing with every bite of food she took and that seemed to take her attention away from what was being discussed at the dinner table.

"You? A fear of heights? We used to always go mountain climbing when you were little," her father said and seemed to get upset.

"I don't know what happened, it suddenly developed," Amaryllis confessed. She immediately felt guilty as now her father would think they would miss out on their trips. That would never happen. She was just trying to save herself from having to spend time with that homewrecker. That homewrecker who had no sense of shame or decency. To think that after everything he had done and after Amaryllis had told him she knew about his affair, he still stayed and ate with them. A person with at least a bit of self-respect would have not stayed for dinner. He thought that if he acted like nothing happened, things would magically go back to normal. Amaryllis felt like running away. She wished the floor would magically open and swallow her up.

When she realised that couldn't happen, she began to quickly eat the remainder of her rice and carrots. She forced as much broccoli as she could down her throat, whilst gulping down some water to wash away the bitter taste of the carrots. James sat there, poking around with his food, and occasionally looking up to throw Amaryllis an aggravated look. She pretended she did not notice and finished her plate. She excused herself and went up the stairs quickly before her uncle dared to suggest other plans for them.

Amaryllis and Derek were walking down the hall to her favourite lesson - mathematics. They walked hand in hand, not caring that the rest of the school was still gossiping about yesterday's scandal. Amaryllis didn't let any of the things that they were saying get to her as she walked confidently with her head held up high. They walked into the classroom and sat next to each other whilst Natalie sat with Isabel at the table behind them. Amaryllis nudged Derek, but he seemed to be lost in his thoughts as he did not respond. She nudged him again, a little bit harder this time but he still seemed to be in another universe. She decided to click her fingers in front of his face. That did it, he whipped his head around. His blue eyes met her eyes and he attempted to smile but it seemed the corners of his mouth did not want to tug upwards. Amaryllis cocked her head to the side.

"What's wrong?" she asked him, but before he could answer, their maths teacher had come in and whistled loudly, silencing all her students. She wrote $y = mx + c$ on the whiteboard and started going through yesterday's homework answers. Amaryllis tried to focus on her work, but her attention kept wavering back to Derek who seemed to be lost in his thoughts again. He hadn't corrected a single question and they were now on question five. What was wrong with him? She ripped a small piece of paper from the corner of her homework sheet and scribbled something down. She passed it to Derek, who read it and wrote something down on it. He was about to pass it back when Mrs Elis called out Amaryllis' name.

"Sorry, what?" Amaryllis looked dumbfounded. Mrs Elis crossed her arms and repeated her question for her favourite student. If it was anybody else, she would have damned them straight to hell. That would be detention after school for two hours for an entire week.

"What is the answer to question nine, Miss Knight?" she repeated smiling. Amaryllis looked down at her sheet. When did they get to question nine? Question nine was the only question she couldn't answer. She had attempted various methods but could not arrive at a logical answer. Thus, she had thrown all her papers full of her attempts to answer the question, into the bin.

"I am not sure," she confessed, making Mrs Elis's smile transform into a look of shock. She put her hand on her chest as if she had been physically hurt. Derek snickered from his seat and Mrs Elis shot him a look of pure repulse.

"Do you know the answer Mr Rome?" she asked, fixing her glasses that had fallen to the tip of her nose. She pushed them up and waited for Derek to answer her question. He stared at his blank sheet, pretending to find the answer he had worked so hard on the night before.

"Ermm $1.5x$," he said nearly inaudibly, sounding nervous. Mrs Elis almost visibly flinched.

"$1.5x$ children? Does that answer seriously make sense to you Mr Rome?" she asked, making the whole class laugh at Derek. Even Amaryllis couldn't help but let out a snicker. Derek tried to look over at Amaryllis' sheet which only made her snicker louder.

"Sorry," she apologised but continued laughing. Soon he was laughing too and it was all well until Mrs Elis decided to slam her maths textbook on her desk.

"SILENCE," she boomed and the whole class went silent. Apart from Natalie and Isabel who were living on a planet of their own. Mrs Elis glared at them so hard Amaryllis was afraid her eyes would fall out of their place. Isabel seemed to notice this because only Natalie's giggles could be heard now.

"Can you believe that-," she was about to finish her sentence when she saw Mrs Elis' red face. Natalie put her hand on her mouth and her eyes grew wide with fear. Mrs Elis took dangerously slow steps towards Natalie, making Natalie sink back in her chair. Derek slapped his hand on his forehead and looked like he was about to utter a prayer to save his twin's life.

"It honestly baffles me how you are at the top of the class, and you never pay attention," Mrs Elis said through clenched teeth. She looked perplexed. Natalie just looked up at her furious teacher with innocent eyes and a toothy smile, showing off her perfect white teeth. Mrs Elis turned around and went to her desk, making Natalie sigh in relief. Derek sighed too as if what would happen to his twin would happen to him too.

"Detention for a week Miss and Mr Rome. After school for one hour each day starting today," Mrs Elis said, making Natalie and Derek groan. Maybe whatever happened to one twin did happen to the other.

The students hurriedly exited their class with their stomachs rumbling like they had been starved for the whole day. Amaryllis put her books in her bag and soon everyone had left except for her crew. Isabel Flipped her perfect curls back and hung her bag on her shoulder.

"I am starving. Where are we eating?" she said, rubbing her flat stomach. Natalie seemed too busy putting her butterfly hair clips in her hair to hear her friend's question.

"What do you mean where?" Amaryllis asked.

"Well, the school food is getting too repetitive and it's Friday, so we are allowed to go out for lunch. I thought we could go and eat at a French restaurant or something," she said. Derek peeked Amaryllis on the cheek and went to meet up with his friends.

"I know an amazing French restaurant and it's so close. It's called Le restaurant and it has the best steak you could ever taste," Amaryllis gushed. Natalie finished putting her gold hair clips on and the trio left the classroom. As they walked down the hallway and out of the school there was an awkward silence. Natalie didn't talk and instead constantly took out her mirror to move her hair clips around, and Amaryllis and Isabel were not exactly best friends. Natalie must have finally taken heed of the awkward silence and decided to speak.

"There it is," Natalie pointed at a place right opposite the school gate. They went through the school gate and crossed the street from the middle of the sidewalk. They looked left and right before they ran but stopped when they saw a car approaching. After the car passed, they continued running until they were on the other side of the road.

They pushed the door and went inside the dimly lit restaurant. The atmosphere was cosy and a waitress welcomed them in. She led them to a table for four people near a big aquarium that was full of colourful fishes. There were small red fishes that looked to be about an inch in size. There were also a couple of bigger fishes that were blue and had colourful pink tales. Many more fishes in different colours and sizes were in the aquarium and there were fake plants and a little castle so the fishes would feel at home like they would in the ocean. At the bottom of the pool, there was a starfish. It was so huge. It was the size of a basketball and even resembled it in its orange colour. The trio took their seats and picked up the menus the waitress had given to them.

Natalie was the first one to speak, "everything looks so delicious," she said as she showed them the pictures of some of the dishes. There was a mouth-watering steak with roasted vegetables and several other tasty dishes from the lunch menu. She turned the page and showed them the dessert section. Her eyes shone when her eyes spotted the pistachio macarons.

"I am so going to order some chocolate and pistachio macarons after I have that steak," Natalie said.

"I am going to have the steak too and chocolate macarons later, but not pistachio macarons. I hate pistachio," Amaryllis said and made a fake gag sound.

Isabel raised an eyebrow, "you hate pistachio macarons? They're like the best."

"I get sick whenever I taste anything pistachio," Amaryllis said. Isabel just gaped at her. After they had decided what they wanted to order, they called the waitress over.

After a while of waiting for their food, they decided to explore the fish aquarium after another waitress gave them a bit of fish food. They threw some fish food in the aquarium and the fish swam as fast as they could to the food. They ate all the food in an instant. However, some fish didn't manage to get any food as they were too small and too weak to battle the bigger fish. Natalie looked at the small ones with sympathetic eyes. She asked for more fish food and threw it to the smaller fish, but the bigger fish fought with them and ate their food.

The sound of plates being placed on a table alerted the trio that their food had been served. Isabel and Amaryllis rushed to the table and started devouring their stake, roasted potatoes and carrots. Meanwhile, Natalie stayed glued to the fish tank and tapped the glass of the aquarium to play with the tiny fish.

"Common the food is so good. We can go to an aquarium another day," Amaryllis called her best friend. Natalie walked from the aquarium and sat down to eat her meal. Picking up her fork, she cut a small bite of her stake and took a bite. She made a disgusted face which she kept on as the waitress came and asked them how the food was. Amaryllis and Isabel expressed how good it was whilst Natalie looked far from pleased.

"Excuse me, this is uncooked. Please tell the chef that he needs to cook his food properly before he serves it to people," Natalie said and held up her plate for the waitress to take it. The waitress looked at her like she was stupid but mastered a fake smile and took the plate to the kitchen. Amaryllis and Isabel stared at Natalie with their mouths falling open.

"What?" Natalie asked as she looked at her two friends.

"They cook them like that on purpose. This is why we came to a French restaurant because they know how to cook their steak," Isabel said.

Natalie looked at Amaryllis for support, but she had already switched her attention back to her plate and continued eating her food. A short moment later, the waitress arrived and set Natalie's plate on the table. Natalie smiled but her smile dropped when she noticed her steak looked the same as it had when it was first served.

"Sorry but the chef says it is cooked properly and he won't cook it any longer," the waitress said and walked away, leaving Natalie angry and hungry. She picked up her fork and stabbed it into the steak. She cut chunks of it and chewed it hard. For the rest of the meal, Natalie's anger level did not change. For once in her life, she had not got what she wanted and she was not happy about it.

Chapter 8

You're Just a Bet

Derek wore a white shirt neatly tucked into his trousers and it was buttoned up until the very last button. His hair was gelled back, and he was having his fourth attempt at tying his black tie. He fiddled with the tie, trying to make a knot or at least that's what he thought he was supposed to do. He had never worn a tie, even at school. He always wondered how he got away without any detentions since Mrs Smith always gave out detentions to people who had not worn their uniform properly.

His phone buzzed with a text message from Amaryllis appearing. "I am so excited," it read. He looked it over, but instead of a smile forming on his face, a look of guilt filled his features.

He tried to tie the stupid tie again, but it wanted to make his life harder. It was as if the tie was telling him to not go on this date. It was as if the tie was telling him to just leave Amaryllis waiting in the restaurant for the second time. He yanked it off and threw it on the floor. The tie certainly deserved this treatment after what it was telling him to do. How dare it tell him to leave Amaryllis? He grumbled something under his breath angrily and took his phone from his black nightstand.

Everything in his room was black, his bed frame, his huge wardrobe that had three double doors, his desk and his nightstand. Only his bed sheets and duvet covers were a contrasting white. The only other colours that could be spotted in his room were blue and red. The blue from his maths and science textbooks and the red from book projects for art.

He shoved his phone into his left pocket and opened the top drawer on his nightstand. He reached his hand inside and pulled out a little red box. He opened the box, looked at the treasure hidden inside and for the first time in a while, smiled. A genuine warm smile. He shoved that into his pocket as well and turned to leave.

Sitting across from him was the woman he was currently having his date with. Derek had not been on a date for over a year. Girls had always begged him for a date, but he was never interested in them. Or at least, not interested in them in that way. He just wanted girls for a one-night stand. He noticed that Amaryllis was beaming brightly at him. He couldn't take this anymore. Soon all the light radiating from her face would vanish after Derek tells her the truth. Derek lowered his gaze and picked up the menu to find something to order that would not take him long to finish. A waiter approached their round table and Amaryllis ordered a few things off the menu. Looks like they would be here for more than he had hoped.

The waiter turned to Derek, "are you ready to order sir?" Derek looked at the waiter, agitated. If he was ready to order he would have called him over.

"Yes, can I have the same order as my date," he said. The waiter scribbled his order down on his small notepad and left.

"I thought you hated chocolate souffle," Amaryllis noted.

"Yes, I do," he said, giving her a look that seemed to wonder if he had said something that indicated otherwise.

"So why did you order it?" she asked her eyebrow arched in question. Derek rubbed the back of his neck.

"I didn't realise you ordered that."

"Oh."

It was now or never. Derek rubbed his sweaty palms on his trousers and pulled out his little red box from his pocket. He held onto the box with a tight grip as if he was afraid it would slip from his hand. Amaryllis was craning her neck to see when the food would come. How beautiful she looked with her strapless red midi dress and her diamond tassel earrings. Her hair was curled and styled so the curls were falling on her bare shoulders. Derek watched as Amaryllis ran her hands through her curls, brushing them out and pushing them behind her shoulder. How he wished he could run his fingers through her curls. He could already imagine how they would feel. They would feel like expensive silk. From the corner of his eyes, Derek thought he saw the figure of somebody familiar. In the distance, he thought he imagined someone walking towards them, waving. But Derek hadn't invited anyone else. This was a date. The figure became clearer and clearer as it approached their table. That toothy grin could not belong to anyone other than his best mate. Nicholas. Derek shoved the box inside his pocket and rubbed his chin, waiting for Nicholas to come.

"Hey, guys. Fancy seeing you here," he laughed and put his hand on Amaryllis' shoulder. He kissed her on the cheek, making Derek's shoulders tense. Picking up a chair from an empty table, he allowed himself to sit at their table.

"We are having a date," Derek said in a harsh voice, stating the obvious. Nicholas' piercing green eyes seemed to pierce into Derek's soul as he looked at him, but he covered his deathly glare with a big smile.

"Oh, am sorry. Am I intruding?" he asked, feigning innocence.

"No, it's fine," Amaryllis said and smiled at Nicholas. Derek wanted to open his mouth and scream at him. Tell him that it wasn't okay and that he needed to go away. Is what he made him do not enough? Could he have not let him have this one night with her alone? Maybe once he explained everything to her, she would understand. Maybe she would forgive him and maybe they could be a real couple. His thoughts were cut short by the food arriving. There were two plates of chocolate souffle, two plates of a vegetarian stew and two small plates of strawberry macarons. Nickolas grabbed one of the chocolate souffle plates and started devouring it. Derek and Amaryllis stared at him unblinking as he munched loudly.

"You hate chocolate. So, I thought I could eat it," he said after he had wiped the plate clean. Derek grunted whilst Amaryllis turned her attention to the vegetable stew and started eating it.

"Garçon, I want to order," Nicholas waved a waiter over. Derek grabbed his hand and pulled it down.

"That's enough. Go to your table," he hissed, bringing his face closer to Nicholas so they were at eye level. Nicholas just smiled and patted Derek on his shoulder.

"Relax. It's not like this is a real date. Did you believe your lie," Nicholas said, the smile on his face seemed to never waver as if it was stuck on his face with super glue. Or maybe he had a condition that prevented him from not smiling. Amaryllis stopped her spoon mid-air and looked at Derek questioningly.

"What does he mean by it's not a real date?" she asked him. Derek ignored Amaryllis and turned his attention back to his friend.

"Go away."

"No," was Nicholas' simple response. Derek wiped the side of his mouth with a napkin, probably forgetting he had yet to eat and dragged Nickolas up from his arm. Nicholas struggled against Derek's iron grip but finally managed to free his hand. His smile finally dropped. He pushed Derek back and Derek pushed him with a greater force causing him to stumble and nearly fall.

"Stop it," Amaryllis cried. They both looked at her as they remembered she was still there. "What did you mean when you said it wasn't a real date?" she asked Nicholas. Derek gulped as he looked at his friend's mischievous smile.

"He's playing you, sweetheart. If he gets a date with you, I buy him a Lamborghini. That was the bet," Nicholas said, emphasising the word Lamborghini as if it was something magnificent. As if it was worth more than her.

His explanation was so straightforward and so simple that it was hard to make sense of it. Amaryllis looked dumbfounded. She seemed to shake her head as if what Nicholas had told her didn't register with her. After a little while, Amaryllis looked at Derek with an expression that was full of mixed emotions. Disgust. Hatred. Betrayal.

She came towards Derek and looked at him from head to toe. Then she scrunched her face up in disgust and raised her hand and slapped him across the face. The sound her hand made when it met his cheek attracted the attention of everyone dining and working at the restaurant. She spun around, grabbed her Prada bag and disappeared out of the restaurant, her silver heels clicking loudly against the floor. Derek stood there looking at the door as if she would come back. But she didn't. The only thing that broke Derek out of his trance was Nicholas' maniacal laughter. It all happened so fast. Derek's fist collided with Nicholas's nose and a cracking sound echoed off the walls of the restaurant. Nicholas cried out in pain, blood spilling from his nose like a waterfall. Looking at Derek in shock, he stumbled and fell to the floor, clutching his broken nose.

"I can't believe my brother would do that," Natalie screeched, her eyes seemed to glow with anger. She stood up from the bench in Flora's Park and made her hands into fists. Isabel rubbed Amaryllis' arm up and down whilst giving her a sympathetic look. Natalie stomped her feet on the fallen green leaves in the park and seemed to act out how she would beat up Derek and pounce him as she made fists with her hands and pretended to pounce on an imaginary figure and punch him senseless. Amaryllis stopped her crying and looked at Natalie's theatre performance with as much of a smile she managed to pull. Isabel gave her a napkin to dry her tears and then pulled Natalie to the bench to calm her down.

"How are you feeling now?" Isabel asked.

"Used. Betrayed. Worthless," Amaryllis answered as she sniffed.

"All boys are the same," Isabel grumbled.

"You know what. Let's not talk about this anymore. Let's shift our attention to something else," Natalie suggested maturely for the first time in her life. Amaryllis nodded but continued sniffing. Her nose was red, and her cheeks were flushed. Her eyes were red and puffy as if she had cried for hours because that is exactly what she had done.

"What I want to know is how are you two finally getting along?" Natalie returned to her nosy self. She wasn't being mature, she just wanted to know something. Isabel shifted uncomfortably on the bench as she looked anywhere but at Natalie. She looked over at the pink blossom trees that decorated Flora Park and Amaryllis seemed to pretend she was distracted by the splinters that were showering the grass and the flowers with water. Natalie fake coughed and tapped each of her friend's shoulders to get their attention.

"The reason why I didn't like Amaryllis before was because I always thought she was entitled and rude, but then I realised that Rose made her look that way and I completely misjudged her," Isabel admitted, her cheeks turning a strong shade of pink. Amaryllis raised her eyebrow.

"You thought I was entitled and rude?" she repeated. Isabel nodded, embarrassment written all over her face.

"Whatever gave you that impression?" she said.

"Rose always made fun of people, of the way they dressed, the way they looked and since you were the only person that hung around with her, I thought you were like her," Isabel said. Amaryllis looked baffled.

"Rose was always so innocent and nice. I never saw her be anything but nice to everyone," Amaryllis said.

"In front of you," Natalie added in. Amaryllis shifted her attention from Derek and Rose to the beautiful nature in the park. Although she had seen these splinters and flowers a hundred times before, they were still a beautiful sight to take in. The beauty of nature always calmed Amaryllis when she was having a stressful or bad day. On the grass in front of her, there were red roses that were made into a heart shape and white roses next to them that were made into another heart shape. Both of these hearts were on the ground and surrounding them were all kinds of different flowers. There were white lilies, pink peonies, blue violets, orange daisies and many more colours and types of different flowers.

Chapter 9

The Hotel Room

Lisa smiled as she sat up in a white double bed. She pulled the white covers off her and climbed out of bed, wearing only her short orange nightgown. She put her blonde hair up in a loose bun and grabbed her phone from the nightstand. Looking through Instagram, she watched a few Instagram stories and scrolled through them one by one. Her heart sank as she saw that James had posted a selfie with that woman. She was the same woman that he had flirted with at the party Lisa had hosted recently. Although Lisa didn't want to admit it, the woman was gorgeous. She had sleek black hair and contrasting emerald eyes that looked prettier than a real emerald would. In the picture, they were both smiling, and he had his arm draped around her shoulder. She clicked on the screen, to see more of his story, and a video of them bowling together came up. The video showed the woman throwing the ball down the lane, making all the pins fall. She ran and hugged James who put his arms around her. Lisa put her hand on her chest and threw her phone at the wall. The phone fell to the ground with a loud thud. A moment later, James came out of the shower, water dripping down his chest and a towel draped around the lower half of his body. He smiled as he used a smaller towel to dry his face and hair.

"What's wrong baby?" he said as he walked towards Lisa. Before he knew it his face whipped to the side from the impact of Lisa's smack and the small towel fell to the floor. He put his hand on his cheek.

"You cheater. Is this what you do to me after I risked my marriage and reputation for you," she screamed and raised her hand to smack him again, but he caught her hand mid-air. Rage flashed in Lisa's eyes. She had decided to cheat on her husband, who was also the father of her only daughter and now her lover had stabbed her in the back. Her head throbbed from the many angry thoughts rushing through her mind. She felt manipulated and used. She also felt stupid for not even suspecting that James would cheat on her. She felt stupid for trusting him.

"What the hell do you mean? I never cheated," he screamed back. Lisa freed her hand from his grasp and paced up and down the room, rubbing her temples and trying to calm down. James noticed Lisa's phone on the floor and went to pick it up. He typed in the password and opened her phone only for his Instagram stories to appear. He gave a booming playful laugh.

"Is this what you are so upset about? She's just a friend," he said and tossed her phone on the bed. He threw himself on the bed and continued drying his dirty blonde hair with another towel he had grabbed from the nightstand.

"Yeah right. That's what all of you say," Lisa snapped back as she went to put her trousers and white t-shirt on. James rubbed the tip of his nose.

"You don't have to worry about her. I only love you and I would never dream of cheating on you. What do you say we eat at this new Chinese restaurant and forget about all of this nonsense?" he said and walked to her. She pushed past him and walked towards the hotel door. She swung the door open and was about to storm out when she saw someone that made her heart drop. A few feet in front of her, stood Richard. He was talking with someone that worked at the hotel and if he had turned his head just a little bit to the side, he would have spotted his wife immediately. She shut the door faster than the speed of lightning and ran inside.

"Can't get enough of me can you," James said, wiggling his eyebrows. Lisa dropped her bag on the floor and covered her mouth with her hand.

"He's here," she said in a whisper.

"Who's here? What's wrong with you today?" he said and walked to the door to open it. Lisa saw this, sprinted towards him and stood in front of the door, blocking it.

"Are you crazy? Do you want us to get exposed?" she hissed. James put his head in his hands.

"Woman why don't you explain something clearly to me for once in your life and tell me who's there," he said, sounding tired. One word would change his face to that of a scared deer and one word would make his heart start racing. One word would make him fear for his life. Only one word.

"Richard. Richard is there," she breathed out. She watched as his face turned yellow, and he sprinted to the hotel closet to change into his boxers, black trousers and blue shirt. Lisa locked the door behind her and found his wallet on the nightstand and tossed it to him.

She opened the terrace door and looked down. There was a good possibility that they could jump and make it out alive, even if they had a few broken bones. They were only on the second floor, not counting the ground floor. James came and looked down, thinking of a possible escape route. He looked at the terrace below them and got an idea. First, they would jump down to the terrace on the floor beneath them, which wasn't hard to do, at least not for him. After they were on the first floor, they would jump into the pool. James started climbing over the terrace.

"What are you doing?" Lisa whispered.

"We need to jump to the terrace below, then we can jump into the pool and then we can get away," he said. Lisa looked at him as if he had gone mad. She shook her head vigorously as James continued with his crazy escape plan. He jumped to the terrace below and cried out in pain as he clutched his knee. Lisa still looked like she would rather exit through the door and started walking towards it. That was before she heard Richard's voice.

"Yes, I want to check the rooms and see if this hotel is something that I might invest in," she heard him say through the door. That's all it took for her to climb over the terrace and jump. She landed on her feet but clutched her hip in pain. Nonetheless, she climbed over the terrace again and jumped into the pool. She gasped for air, breathing in water instead. She felt her lungs fill with water and she swam towards the surface as fast as she could. When she got to the surface, James pulled her out. She gasped for air and started coughing harshly. Some people that were sunbathing near the pool were watching them, whispering and giggling.

"These people might recognise me," she said in-between coughs and climbed out of the pool.

"Trust me no one would recognise you when you're wearing cheap, unbranded clothes,' he said and tittered. Lisa shot him an annoyed look as she sat drenched next to the pool, coughing the water out of her system. She felt James drag her up by her arms and they ran towards the exit of the hotel, leaving behind footprints of water. They positioned themselves on James' motorcycle. He put his key in and turned his motorcycle on. He was ready to take off when Lisa's next words made him turn his head around so fast Lisa was afraid his neck would snap.

"I forgot my bag in the hotel room."

Chapter 10

You Used To Be Different

Everyone's phone buzzed and they pulled their phones outs, checking the message that had interrupted their important conversations. Their important conversations included listing the number of houses, horses and even boats their parents owned. It also included where they would spend their summer holiday. Would it be Miami? Or, somewhere in Europe like France or Spain? For the girls, their conversations also included any shopping trips they were planning this weekend and whether it was in France or Italy.

The students watched their phone screens in fascination. They started murmuring and snickering, looking in Amaryllis' direction. Amaryllis turned her head around to face Natalie who just sat there, a sympathetic look on her face. Her hand covered her mouth, although it wasn't clear if that was a result of shock or to stop herself from telling everything to her best friend. Amaryllis opened her phone and went to their year's group chat. There was a picture of a letter written by hand in red ink. It was from an unknown number.

It read, "Stupid girls never learn. They run after the same boy again and again. Even if it means them ending up as a bet for them. Stupid girls never learn. That's why they are called stupid. In our case the stupid girl is Amaryllis, and the boy that made the bet is Derek." That messy and sloppy handwriting only belonged to one person.

Amaryllis slammed her phone on the table, uttering only one word, "Rose." She dialled a number and put her phone to her ear. Ever since that day, she had deleted his number from her contacts. She tapped her fingers on the table impatiently, but no one picked up. She dialled his number again and as soon as he answered the call, she screamed through the phone, causing everyone to jump in their seats.

"How dare you tell her what you did to me, you imbecile?" Natalie swiftly made a go for Amaryllis' phone and managed to wrestle it out from her hands. Natalie struggled with her hold on the phone. She tossed it from one hand to the other until she had control over it. By the time she looked at the screen, Derek had already hung up. Amaryllis' eyes flashed with annoyance and her chest heaved up and down.

"You must control yourself. Don't give people something else to talk about. You don't want more gossip about you," Natalie warned. Amaryllis closed her eyes and her breathing slowly calmed down.

"You are right I need to calm down. It's probably Nate or Derek that spread the news. But I also know who wrote that letter," Amaryllis said, her eyes scanning the room and falling on the table nearest to the door. Natalie followed her gaze and her eyes landed on a girl that was filing her nails and humming a happy melody. Natalie's eyes sparkled with mischief. She clapped her hands together and rubbed them excitedly. Natalie stood up on her feet and so did Amaryllis. They were getting ready to make their way to Rose's table when the door was suddenly torn open, and Mrs Elis stormed in. Her eyes were red and puffy, and she was carrying a huge stack of papers in one hand and her coffee in the other. Natalie and Amaryllis sat back down on their chairs as Mrs Elis made her way to her desk. She slammed her papers on her desk, attracting the attention of every student in the room. That silenced them. They hid their phones. The boys hid them in their trouser pockets and the girls hid them in their skirt pockets. Mrs Elis looked at every single student in the room, her gaze lingering on Amaryllis the longest. Her eyes narrowed and Amaryllis found herself worrying about Mrs Elis' eyes. She looked like she had an eye problem. Amaryllis foolishly raised her hand to tell Mrs Elis just that. Mrs Elis scoffed but allowed Amaryllis to speak regardless.

"Miss you might want to go to a doctor and get your eyes checked. They're red and you seem to squint them a lot," she said. Mrs Elis scoffed again and laughed. It wasn't a funny laugh; it was a laugh laced with sarcasm and irritation.

"I don't have an eye problem. I have been crying my eyes out. I have spent hours and hours teaching you and making extra revision sessions for you to consolidate your knowledge of the material you should have learnt. I have also lost so many nights' sleep marking your tests and choosing the questions so carefully as to not make them too easy or too hard. I thought this was an easy test you see. But how wrong I was. You all failed the tests you see, apart from one student," she said whilst holding up her index finger to emphasise her point that only one student had passed the test. Amaryllis had a smug look on her face that was soon wiped off her face by Mrs Elis delivering the shocking news.

"You're not the student that passed Amaryllis. It was Natalie," she said in disbelief, whilst motioning to Natalie who was busy painting her nails pink. She made sure to select the exact shade of pink as her bow hair clip, which she wore on the left side of her head. Natalie looked up slowly, stopping her manicure session.

"What?" Natalie asked, oblivious to her long teacher's rant.

"You are the only one that passed the test," Mrs Elis repeated, smacking her hand on her thigh.

"Why is everyone so surprised? I always get top grades," she said whilst looking at everyone's shocked faces including Amaryllis' face. "I am seriously very offended right now."

Amaryllis pointed her index finger at herself, "I failed? That's impossible. I have never failed. There has to be some kind of mistake. I need to check the marks myself," she said, not seeming to accept the simple fact that she had failed. She blinked her eyes several times to make sure that this was reality and not a horrible nightmare and approached Mrs Elis' desk. She flipped through the huge pile of papers until she found hers. She snatched her paper from the file, whilst Mrs Elis threw herself on her chair and buried her head in her hands. She flipped through the pages, her eyes scanning the pages to find the total mark for each question. She looked at the bottom of each page and saw mostly zeros. She gasped louder and louder as she went through the test. Some pages had a few marks on them, which meant that she wasn't completely brainless. Thank the heavens.

A loud giggle broke her out of her trance. She slammed her paper on the desk and glared daggers at Rose, who was pretending to muffle her giggles by covering her mouth with her hand. She felt her blood boil and her heart start to beat faster. The anger she felt told her to go and give her a taste of her own medicine, but the peaceful part of her told her to stay calm. She didn't also need a bad reputation after she failed her mathematics test. However, sometimes the peaceful part of a person loses the battle. Amaryllis found herself striding across the room to Rose's desk. She grabbed her by the hair, locking each of her fingers around her rough lion mane hair. For a moment, Amaryllis was afraid for her delicate skin but then she remembered all that Rose had done to her. First, she showed everyone her crush scrapbook and made her look like a love lunatic and then she had spread the news that Derek started dating her just to win a bet. Rose cried out in pain and dug her nails in Amaryllis' skin, but Amaryllis seemed to tighten her hold on her hair as she re-lived through each memory of what Rose had done to her. A few students came to Rose's rescue, but Amaryllis pushed them away. Mrs Elis' voice boomed but Amaryllis could not hear what she was saying. Soon hands were draped around Amaryllis' waist, trying to pull her away from Rose. She tried to push the person away, but it seemed they were adamant about rescuing the ugly duckling. Natalie pried Amaryllis' hands off Rose's bush hair. Amaryllis sent her friend a betrayed look to which Natalie just rolled her eyes.

"You'll get in trouble," Natalie defended her traitorous actions. Mrs Elis led Amaryllis to her chair and whistled loudly for everyone to stop talking. The only sounds that could be heard were Rose's muffled cries. Her shoulders shook violently, and she was attempting to straighten her nightmare hair out. She was unsuccessful. With every stroke of her fingers, her hair poked out more, making her look like a witch.

"What has happened to you? You used to have top grades, you used to be so kind to everyone," Mrs Elis raved on and on about how Amaryllis had changed. If only she took a moment to think about why she had changed. If only she thought about what she might be going through to cause her to act this way. But people never cared enough to question why. They loved when a person did something wrong. They secretly loved it. They loved pointing it out as it somehow made them feel better about the demons that they were hiding in their closet. No one was an angel. Everyone had done something that they were not proud of. Yet instead of admitting their faults and changing their bad habits, they judged someone else's faults. Anyone whose faults were out in the open. However, people often forget that hidden faults were no less wrong than exposed faults.

Amaryllis was given an hour of detention after school today. At least she wouldn't be alone. She would join Natalie and the man that ruined her life in their detention. Thankfully, she would not be joining them with the detentions that they had for the rest of the week. Sighing, she stomped down the hallway and shoved her shoulder past Derek, causing him to nearly slam into his locker. He turned around and opened his mouth to most likely scream at his assaulter but closed it shut when he saw it was Amaryllis.

Natalie trotted down the hall by her side, making sure to keep a good distance between them. Anyone could sense the fury radiating off Amaryllis. Natalie looked at Amaryllis from the corner of her blue eyes. She fiddled with her hair as she watched her friend's angry facial expression dissolve into an emotionless one.

"Watch it," Amaryllis sneered as she shoved past another student. The girl who had red pigtails looked down at the ground, her lip quivering and ran down the hall in the same direction she had come from. Natalie called a sorry after her and gave a disapproving look to her friend. What was happening to her? She never took her anger out on innocent people. She had never raised her voice at anyone before. Whereas now, she was pushing people and talking down to them. She took a second look at Amaryllis' face. It lacked any emotion. No one could guess how she was feeling or what she was thinking. She might as well be a walking robot or a statue.

"Wait, where are we going? English is that way," Natalie called after her friend who preceded to go in the direction of the school exit. Amaryllis stopped walking, her back still turned back to Natalie.

"I am not going. I am going shopping," Amaryllis snapped. Natalie looked like she had been slapped across the face.

"Ok, you know what. I have had enough of your attitude. Don't take your anger out on me or anybody else. If you want to take it out on somebody, take it out on Derek or Rose. They would be in English class right now," Natalie said, raising her index finger and pointing it at Amaryllis like she was a parent telling off her six-year-old child. Amaryllis' hard and emotionless expression seemed to soften a little bit.

"You are right. I am sorry," she said and went to hug her friend.

One of the maids who was wearing a white shirt tucked into a black pencil skirt set the dinner plates down in front of Amaryllis, Richard, Lisa and of course James. His visits had become so frequent that one would think he lived with them.

Amaryllis took in the smell of lasagne that filled the room. She reached for the serving utensil and put a piece of lasagne on her plate. Digging her fork into the cheesy dish, she took her first bite and chewed the soft meat in delight and closed her eyes as she continued chewing it. The maid put down four glasses of white wine to her delight. She sipped from her glass and then started gulping it down.

Her father put his hand on the glass, lowering it from her mouth, "slowly, slowly," he said.

"Thank you for the food, Lisa it's delicious," James joked. Lisa gave a fake little laugh but gave him a quick dirty look from the corner of her eyes. Amaryllis mimicked her mother as she ate a mouthful of her lasagne. Richard seemed to be the only one to find humour in the joke and laughed.

"How was your trip honey?" Richard asked making Lisa choke on her food. James reached his hand and patted her back, but Lisa just swayed away in her seat and chucked down some water.

"Emm, it was great. Paris was wonderful," she said. Richard studied his wife, his hand rubbing his chin.

"It's just that I think I found your bag in the Maria hotel yesterday," he said. He reached his hand to the seat next to him and pulled up a scrunched up bright green bag. He held it up in the air in front of his wife so she could see it. Lisa chuckled nervously and tried to reach over her food to take it, but Richard pulled it away from arm's reach. He seemed to inspect it and then decided to give it to his wife. Richard waited for an explanation as to how his wife could be at two places at the same time. Lisa tucked a strand of her blonde hair behind her ear and sat up straighter in her seat.

"So, you didn't go to Paris? I don't understand," Richard asked.

"I visited a friend in the hotel after I came back from Paris. She came here from Spain. I haven't seen her in years, so I was beside myself. I must have forgotten my bag there," Lisa explained.

Richard clicked his tongue, looking at Lisa. He took his eyes off her and continued eating his food. Lisa reached for her wine glass and screamed for the maid to refill it, although it was still half full. James sat there with his head down, eating his lasagne as quick as he could. Once he finished, he wiped the side of his mouth with a tissue. But before he could escape, Richard had cut another piece of lasagne and put it on his plate. He looked like a deer caught in red headlights with his big confused eyes meeting his brother's amused ones. Smiling, Richard told his brother to eat more.

"You haven't eaten much. If you continue like this, you'll get sick. Look how skinny you are. I have noticed you haven't been eating much lately," Richard said, pointing to his brother's body. Amaryllis didn't know what her mother saw in James. He looked skinny to the point where, if he lost a few pounds, he would only be skin and bones. His blonde hair was always a mess and he never bothered to brush it. His clothes were always dirty, from climbing up mountains and visiting forests to take photographs for his work. Amaryllis could not deny that he was a great photographer. That was one of two things that might have attracted her mother to him. His pictures made Amaryllis feel as if she was in the place that the camera had captured. His pictures made her feel alive. Free even.

The only other good thing she could find about him was that he was handsome. One could not deny that he had the face of an angel, all the girls swooned over him wherever he went. Amaryllis had to experience envy and jealousy from random girls as they thought she was his girlfriend. Whenever she went with him to a public place like a café, all the girls would be talking and whispering about her. They would make fun of how she looked and even how she spoke. His photographs and his looks were the only two good things about him. Apart from that, there was nothing else. He wasn't even rich. That was one of the most important things in her mother's life. Money. Otherwise, what would she do with herself if she could not fly first class? Or, if she had to cook her food? Or, if she had to do her laundry? What was her mother going to do, leave her dad and live in a cottage with her uncle? She could never live like that. A few days and she would pass away from shock or depression.

Amaryllis was bought back to reality with the doorbell ringing. After Lisa had screamed three times for someone to get the door, one of the maids had rushed to open it. Amaryllis tried to listen to their conversation to find out who was at the door at this time of day, but her ears didn't catch a word of what they were saying. It was eight o'clock in the evening. Who would come at this time to someone's house unannounced? After speaking to someone at the door, the maid came rushing in. She was fiddling with her apron and shuffling on her feet, "Mr Knight the police are at the door." There was a moment of silence before Richard pushed his chair out and rushed up to the door. Amaryllis followed behind him and Lisa and James followed behind her.

"Good evening, Mr Knight. I am sorry to tell you that Mr Andrews managed to break into Smith High School again and unfortunately, he has killed someone." They all looked at each other and then at the officer. One question was taunting them all, whom did he kill?

Chapter 11

Mr Andrews Again

"Wait, I just want to talk to you. I just want to explain everything," Derek shouted after Amaryllis as she rushed past the shops. Her eyes scanned the shops rapidly and the clothes inside them as she continued her escape.

She was carrying a dozen Louis Vuitton shopping bags in her hands. Some were big, some were small. The weight of those bags slowed her down and soon he got a hold of her hand and she was facing him.

"There's nothing to explain. You were an absolute jerk," she shouted back in his face, stealing her hand away from his grasp.

She wore a white mini pleated skirt with white trainers and a nude short-sleeved top. Her hair was curled and her curls bounced whenever she turned around or walked.

She spun on her heel and walked into her next destination - Zara. Before she could process what had happened, she was lifted off the ground and her legs hung in the air. She kicked her legs back on his stomach and screamed to be let down, but his grip around her waist only tightened. Her screaming attracted the attention of the shoppers and they watched the scene with horror. A few men and women came to reason with Derek and tell him to put her down. One man wearing a long black coat seemed very adamant. He treated him cautiously as if he was a kidnapper and was afraid he would hurt Amaryllis. He told him he would not call the police if he put her down. He could have been imagining things, but he bet his life he heard Amaryllis snicker silently. There were a few girls from their school that took this golden opportunity and filmed the scene. They would later post that on their social media accounts and gossip about it. Derek could already imagine the rumours they would make up. He imagined that one rumour would say that Derek was abusing Amaryllis. Whereas, another rumour would say that Amaryllis threw herself in his arms because she was a crazy love lunatic. Seeing more people approach him to free Amaryllis, there was only one thing he could do.

"Guys are you being serious? This is my thirteen-year-old sister. Don't let the makeup fool you, it does wonders in making her look older than she is. I am just trying to take her home. She went out without telling our mother and now she is worried sick about her. I have been looking for her for hours, thinking that something might have happened to her," Derek said, pointing at Amaryllis' face which was apparently filled with makeup. The only thing she had applied was a bit of pink lip-gloss and mascara. Wiping away some non-existent tears from his eyes, Derek gave a fake sniff increasing his acting skills from a solid 8 to a 10 very easily. Some adults went back to their shopping and one woman offered him a napkin, which he took and wiped his eyes with.

His eyes were red and puffy from staying up all night yesterday. Thus, it wasn't that hard to fool them into thinking that he was crying. He had stayed up all night studying for the exams. Derek had never taken studying seriously and succeeded in failing every class. However, this was serious. This was his future. He had suddenly realised that with the end of year high school exams coming up, his future was on the line. If he wanted to be with Amaryllis, she wouldn't be with someone that didn't have a future ahead of them. He had to at least pass his exams so that he could go to a decent university and pursue a degree that led to good money. He knew Amaryllis always got top grades. She would go to a good university like Oxford or Cambridge and make millions if not billions after graduating. He had to do the same.

Amaryllis screeched loudly as her Louis Vuitton shopping bags fell to the floor after Derek threw her over his shoulder. He retrieved the five bags and carried them.

"He's lying I am not his sister. And I am most definitely not thirteen! Why is everyone so stupid nowadays?" she yelled and pounded her fists on his hard rock back as he carried her out of Zara. Amusement covered everybody's faces and soon the rest of the shoppers had left the scene. Women looked at clothes and men stood next to them, holding their shopping bags while blindly nodding and smiling at every piece they showed them. As if they knew what was fashionable or not. To avoid any problem, they said everything was nice.

Amaryllis and Derek continued their journey through the shopping centre and to his green Lamborghini. Amaryllis looked up and brushed her hair out of her face. She peeked into Bershka and hoped she would spot a few garments she liked but Derek was moving too fast. She kept looking as they passed by more shops, but her head started hurting from looking upside down. She gave up and slumped her body against his back, her curls falling all over her face. A few shops later, they arrived at his Lamborghini. He put her down on the passenger seat and put her bags on the floor near her feet. Derek jumped into his seat and started his dream car up. He felt Amaryllis continuously shift in her seat. She moved further down to the left end of the seat and then to the right end. She crossed her legs then she put her leg down. Her hands fidgeted with the seat belt then she put them on her lap.

"What's wrong?" he asked.

"What's wrong?" she repeated, batting her eyelashes at him to mimic his innocent expression. "Don't you have any shame putting me in the car that you traded me with."

Derek slumped his shoulders and turned the engine off. He licked his lips, "I told you I would explain everything, but not here. Let's go and have a bite. How about that restaurant we went to last time?"

Amaryllis sat frozen in her seat. "And will Nicholas be there?" she said sarcastically. She crossed her arms and cocked her head to the side, waiting for his answer. Derek reached over to Amaryllis, making her shuffle to the other end of her seat. He grabbed the seatbelt and pulled the shoulder strap across her body. Her breath hitched as their faces were inches away from each other. He noticed her tension and locked his ocean blue eyes onto hers. He seemed to stare right into her soul. His staring was so intense, so full of emotion that she felt so exposed to him. She felt...naked. She could smell his minty breath and unconsciously leaned closer to him. He looked at her surprised but leaned his face closer. Their lips were a mere inch away from each other. Suddenly, all the memories came rushing back to her. How he betrayed her and used her although he knew that she had just survived a horrible incident. He knew that Mr Andrews had abused her and tried to kill her and he couldn't have picked a worse time than that to play her. She turned her head to the side, destroying their intimate moment before it could lead to something. He inserted her seat belt into the seat belt buckle and restarted his engine.

Derek stopped his car in front of the Seafood restaurant. It was a white restaurant, decorated with fake seashells all over the door and the windows. Amaryllis looked up and smiled but quickly hid her smile when Derek turned to unbuckle his belt. The Seafood restaurant was her favourite restaurant. If there was anything she loved more than French food it was seafood. Lobsters, fish and prawns were her favourites to eat.

"I know you love this restaurant. Let's go and eat something," he said as he stuffed his key into the pocket of his jeans. He was wearing mid-blue jeans and a black v neck t-shirt. Derek walked meanwhile Amaryllis plodded up the steps of the restaurant. As soon as they went through the door, they could see the fish aquarium on the right side of the restaurant. It was filled with tiny blue and red fish. There were rocks and fake plants to entertain the fish. On the left side were the reservation desk and a statue of a big lobster that held a knife and a fork. The lobster had its tongue sticking out as if it was ready to devour a big meal.

"Welcome Mr Rome. We have reserved the table with the ocean view for you, just as you requested," a waitress said. She wore a white dress and had a mini blue apron tied around her waist. The usual staff uniform was a blue pencil skirt with a matching blue t-shirt and a white apron. This girl might be the manager or she might be someone that has a higher work status than the rest of the staff. However, one could tell she was no older than eighteen and usually the manager in this restaurant was either in their thirties or forties.

"Thank you. Come let's go, I know you love the ocean," he said, taking her hand in his. Amaryllis tried to free her hand from his tight grip but he just tightened his hold. The waitress showed them to their table and told them that the food he had requested would be arriving soon. Amaryllis looked in awe at the view before her eyes. Although she had seen the view more than a hundred times before but there was no ocean bluer than this. It was so clear and beautiful. She watched as the waves hit the beach shore and instantly felt her toes curl in delight. How she longed to walk on the sands of the beach and splash her feet in the water. How she wanted to swim in the ocean and swim to the deeper parts of it where she could see all the sea creatures that lived there. She wanted to see the fishes, starfishes, turtles and so many more. There were teenage boys and girls some of whom were playing volleyball and some of whom were sunbathing. Some sat in the sand and built sandcastles and the rest were playing in the ocean and splashing water at each other.

The sound of someone tapping their foot on the floor snapped Amaryllis out of her thoughts. She had forgotten that Derek was sitting right there. A scowl masked his tired face.

"I was asking you if you were okay. I texted you yesterday but you didn't reply. I heard that Mr Andrews killed your art teacher," he said.

"I am fine. I didn't have a close relationship with Ms Emma. She barely even spoke to me. I just hope Mr Andrews gets the death penalty so we can finally feel safe. Otherwise, he will just escape from prison again and kill someone else. And I blocked your number because I don't want to speak to you so I didn't see any of your messages," she said. Ms Emma was also one of her father's assistants at his company. She used to work as an art teacher in the morning and as an assistant in the afternoon. Amaryllis could see the sadness in her father's eyes when the police told him about her death.

"Well, I am glad you are okay. As I said before I wanted to explain everything. Maybe when you know everything you will forgive me and we can start over," he said.

Silence.

"At the start, I didn't have any feelings towards you and I made the bet. It was a huge mistake. But later on, I started liking you and I was going to call the bet off and tell you everything. But it was too late because Nicholas came and ruined everything," he said, rubbing the back of his neck.

Silence.

"Aren't you going to say something? Anything?" he asked but Amaryllis just switched her attention to the plates of seafood that were served. The first plate was a pasta prawn dish with tomato and basil. The second plate in front of her had a big lobster with a bit of a side salad. She twirled her fork around her pasta and pierced her fork into the prawn. They tasted heavenly. She licked her lips in delight. This was the best pasta dish she had ever eaten. She signed in content and moved the pasta dish to the side. She moved the lobster dish towards her and took a bite of her lobster. It tasted perfect as always and it was so spicy. Amaryllis loved spicy food. This was a sign for her to try new dishes instead of ordering the lobster every time she came. Apart from the amazing food, the restaurant looked very nice. It had big glass windows all around the restaurant, making people feel like they were eating outside near the ocean. The restaurant had white tables and chairs. All the plates they served food with were blue and the cutlery was silver. It was close to the shopping centre Amaryllis always went to and so every time she went shopping she ate there.

  Derek tapped his foot on the floor again. Amaryllis continued eating her lobster, not heeding any attention to the man sitting across from her.

  "Amaryllis talk to me," he begged, running his hands down his face.

  She set her fork down, "what you are telling me is that you played me right after someone tried to kill me." Derek nodded slowly, not knowing what else to do.

  "What you are telling me is that you didn't care about the shock I was going through and said oh hey let's break her even more," she said, waving her hand in the air. Derek readjusted himself on his seat, looking anywhere but at her. His eyes looked to be glued to the floor, whilst her eyes seemed like they were shooting fire at him. Fire that came from the depths of hell.

  "And now you want me to understand that and forgive you. I mean I certainly do understand that you are a jerk and that you don't care about anyone's feelings as long as you get what you want. I could never forgive an egocentric, selfish person like you," she said and with that, she got up and left him sitting there all alone.

Rose huffed as she set down the last box on her bed. She examined her new room. The bed was made of wood that looked a hundred years old and the walls were painted an ugly grey colour. The room was small and only fit a single bed and a small wardrobe. Apart from that, there was barely any walking space. She left her room to inspect the remainder of her house or should she say cottage. Even a cottage would be bigger than this. She knew she should have never trusted her mother. No bank would make a mistake and stop someone's credit card. She should have believed the instincts that told her they were broke. Even now her mother had never stopped lying.

"We will go back to our house as soon as the problem with our company is sorted," she had said. By the time they had moved half of their belongings and furniture to the new house, Rose had had more tantrums than a four-year-old child would have had in two months. Rose knew the truth. They were bankrupt. Only in her dreams could she now afford a Louis Vuitton bag. Only in her wildest dreams will she be able to eat at the expensive restaurants she used to go to with her mother and the ones she used to go to with Amaryllis. Thank God her mother had already paid the fees for her school. Otherwise, she would have needed to go to a community school. How disgraceful. She was also thankful that she wore a uniform. If they didn't have one and she needed to wear her clothes, everyone would realise she was poor if she wore the same designer shoes and clothes she already had every day. They would also realise she was poor if she didn't have any pieces from the new season. Why did this have to happen to her? Why couldn't this happen to Amaryllis? She had everything. Looks, grades, friends, and everyone liked her, even Derek. Why did she have to have money too? Why did her life always have to be perfect? Rose took a seat on her bed and she felt herself sink. She inspected her bed only to find the wood starting to break. She kicked it angrily, causing it to break even more. Leaving her little cage and coming down the stairs, she saw her mother struggling to carry the chairs for the dining table through the door.

"Even my bed is broken. How do you expect me to live like this," Rose screamed at her mother. The tired woman set the chairs down in the hallway and wiped the sweat that formed on her forehead with her shirt sleeve.

"Can't you see that I am struggling and getting all of our stuff to our new house all by myself. The least you could do is not complain since you are not even helping," her mother said as calmly as she could, but inside her blood was boiling.

"I don't care! You are the reason why we are in this mess," Rose screamed.

"Darling calm down," her mother said, placing her hands on Rose's shoulders.

"Move away from me. I hate you. Did you hear me? I hate you. Now everyone I know is going to laugh at me because I am poor. For the past few weeks, I have counted every pound I spent on lunch at school whilst Amaryllis and her friends have been going to expensive French restaurants and buying Prada and Louis Vuitton bags," she screamed the last bit much louder, swatting her mother's hands away from her shoulders.

"You know what shut up. You are such a spoilt brat," her mother screamed back. Rose flinched and stood glued to the floor. Her mother had never raised her voice at her let alone insult her. Rose stormed up the stairs, occasionally turning back around to see if her mother was going to call her back and apologise. The stairs creaked louder with every step she took until she reached the top of the staircase and her mother had still not called her back to apologise.

Chapter 12

Kristina or Katerina

Two girls who were once best friends approached each other from opposite directions of the hallway. One wore black Prada shoes. The other wore black ballet flats from a store that no one would recognise. The students standing near their blue lockers muttered and whispered insults at her cheap and outrageous attire. Rose avoided the urge to burst out in tears and continued her walk of shame. She had always worn her Prada shoes to school, but they didn't fit her anymore, and she didn't have enough money to buy anything but the twelve-dollar shoes she found in a store near her new home.

It was a shoe store with cheap-looking flats and trainers. Half of them had holes in them, and the other half were previously owned by other people. A look of distaste filled her features for the whole of her visit. After looking at the shoes, not daring to touch them or try them on, Rose initially settled on a simple pair of plain black flats that looked decent compared to the rest of the shoes. They only had a scratch on the side.

Snapping out of her daze, Rose noticed a pair of Prada shoes come to a stop in front of her and looked up only to find her ex-best friend. Squinting her eyes, her chubby hands formed into fists by her side. Amaryllis gazed at her shoes, making Rose's feet take a step back. Amaryllis manoeuvred around her and continued her journey. Rose undid her fists and whipped her body around. Her lips pressed tightly together; a feeling of hatred filled her chest. She breathed heavily, hoping to diminish the weight of hatred and tension on her chest but nothing vanished. With the heavy burden of hate, she found herself catching up to Amaryllis. Rose grabbed her hand and forced Amaryllis to face her.

"Don't you dare go past me after giving me that look. I saw how you looked at my shoes. Not everyone wants to wear expensive things. Some of us prefer shoes from the high street instead of wasting our money on shoes from Prada," Rose practically screamed. Amaryllis shifted her gaze to Rose's grip on her hand and tried to free herself from her captive, but she failed miserably.

"You are delusional. I don't care what you wear. I don't care whether you wear an outfit made of diamonds or recycling paper. Now Let me go," Amaryllis demanded, annoyance filling her voice.

"No," Rose said tightening her hold on Amaryllis' hand. Amaryllis cried out in pain and struggled against Rose's hold. Rose was now digging her fingernails into Amaryllis' bare skin. To Amaryllis' luck, Derek came from around the corner and noticed the state Amaryllis was in. He rushed to her and pried Rose's hands off her.

"If you were a man, I would have punched you in the face. You are lucky you are a woman. This is the last time I see you near Amaryllis. Go away before you see another side of me," he said, his ocean blue eyes revealing just how angry he felt. His eyes betrayed his mouth. His usual light blue eyes had darkened into a dark blue and the sparkle in his eyes had gone. It seemed as if he was ready to punch Rose after what she did to his love. He rubbed Amaryllis' hand, noticing a red mark where Rose had gripped her and dug her fingernails in. When Rose didn't move and just examined them, her eyes cold and unblinking, he screamed at her, making her yelp. With mischievous eyes, Amaryllis watched Rose run away like a scared deer.

Derek put his hand under her chin and lifted her face so her eyes could meet his. Her blue eyes looked into his ocean blue eyes. She always got lost in his eyes, they were like the endless ocean. The different shades of blue in them looked like the different shades that the ocean waves would turn as the sun rose and set above the horizon. There were light blue shades, mid-blue shades and other shades of blue that she had never seen before. She pinched herself on her arm, to snap herself out of her half-conscious state.

"Are you ok?" he asked, his hand now holding her chin delicately as if she was a glass vase that might break under too much pressure.

"Yes," she said and attempted to walk away but Derek put his hand around her waist to stop her escape. It seemed everyone thought they had a right to physically stop her from moving.

"Amaryllis don't do this. Don't treat me like this. I am suffocating. I need you to talk to me. Please say anything. Anything," he begged her more with his eyes than his words. Amaryllis' hard expression softened a little bit but hardened again like a stone.

"What do you want me to say. I have nothing to say to you. You lied to me and used me and because of you, everyone started laughing and gossiping about me. They started calling me stupid and they started saying that I was an easy target," she said.

"I know, and I am sorry about that. What can I do to fix things? What can I do to make you forgive me? Tell me. I will do anything," Derek begged. Amaryllis remained silent for a moment as if she was considering Derek's pleas and was thinking of a possible way he could amend things.

"Honestly, there is nothing you can do. You ruined everything between us the moment you made that bet. You broke my trust. I could never trust you again even if I wanted to. Maybe if you didn't keep the car and you told me about everything before Nicholas did, things would have been different," she finally said.

"I'll sell the car. I don't care about the stupid car. As for telling you, I wanted to tell you everything, but Nicholas beat me to it. The only thing I want right now is for you to forgive me," he said.

"It's too late," and with that she walked away, leaving a heartbroken Derek standing alone in an empty hallway.

The doorbell rang during dinner again, filling the air with tension and a sense of Deja vu. Mr Knight went up to answer the door before Lisa had a chance to start screaming at the maids to open it. Richard couldn't handle any loud noise. He was tired as he had spent many hours at work. He also only had one assistant now, meaning he had to do more of the work himself.

Amaryllis and Lisa eyed the door suspiciously. They heard Richard talk with someone and took note that it was a female from the soft voice. However, they couldn't guess who. The voice didn't sound familiar at all. Richard took a step back, allowing the stranger to step into his home. A pair of red high heels stepped forward in the hallway. Slim long legs accompanied them, and the guest took a few more steps in, allowing Amaryllis and Lisa to have a full view of the woman that had interrupted their dinner time. She had porcelain skin that was whiter than snow and hair that was fairer than the sun itself. Her hair was gelled back, and she wore a black mini dress that hugged her body in all the right places. Her hips were wide, but her waist was small. It was obvious from her features that this woman was not from California. She had to be from a country in Scandinavia such as Sweden or Norway. Her cold sharp features were another piece of evidence to support that assumption. The woman took a deep breath, and it was as if all the air in the room was sucked out because suddenly Amaryllis felt like she couldn't breathe. How could someone be this breathtaking? Lisa seemed to be the first of the two to snap out of their trance and looked at her husband in confusion. Richard tore his eyes off the beauty and invited her to sit with them at dinner. He called the maid and told her to set a plate up for another person. Immediately, the maid came rushing in with a plate and some cutlery. Lisa still looked at her husband for an explanation whilst examining the woman from head to toe.

"This is Kristina, she's Emma's, eh I mean Ms Anderson's sister, who was my assistant and Amaryllis' art teacher," Richard introduced his wife and daughter to their uninvited guest. "Kristina this is my daughter, Amaryllis, she used to be one of Ms Anderson's students, and this is my wife, Lisa." Amaryllis muttered a shy hello which Kristina gave a flashing smile.

"And what is she doing here?" Lisa said, looking at Kristina with narrowed eyes. Kristina gave a little laugh that sounded like a beautiful melody. This only made Lisa's jaw tighten more. Richard gave a look to his wife that most likely asked her to be polite.

"I am here to visit Mr Knight. I know that my sister worked as his assistant, and I guess I just wanted him to tell me how she was in her last few months. I had not spoken to her in over a year and now I regret that, now that she's gone," Kristina said, wiping her left eye for the tear that had escaped. Her voice was melodic even when it was sad and the tear that escaped shone like a diamond under the illuminating chandelier. Amaryllis wanted to reach her hands out and catch the tear to inspect it and see if it really could be a diamond. Without consciously realising, Amaryllis had already reached her hands out towards Kristina. Kristina moved back in her seat and cocked her head sideways with one of her eyebrows raised. For a moment, everyone looked at Amaryllis and she looked at her hands, wanting to withdraw them but feeling like she was frozen like a statue.

"Amaryllis, what are you doing?" her mother hissed, and to Amaryllis' luck, pushed her hands down. Amaryllis sighed as if she was saved from committing treason and laughed nervously. There was nothing she could say to explain the crazy idea she had thought of. Instead, she picked up her fork and played around with her lobster and vegetables.

"It's fine. I get that all the time whenever I come to visit California. People don't believe my hair is real and want to touch it to see if it is. They're unused to people with extremely fair hair. But in Sweden it's normal," Kristina smiled. Relief washed over Amaryllis as she didn't have to tell the truth about her strange act. Everyone looked like they had been hit by an arrow from cupid and seemed to have fallen in love with the smallest things Kristina did. Whenever she flipped her hair back or spoke or even breathed, she seemed to have everyone's undivided attention. Apart from Lisa's attention. If only Amaryllis could focus on her maths lessons and study in the same way, she would not have failed that test.

"If you don't mind me asking Mr Knight, how was my sister in the last few months whilst working for you? Was she happy?" she asked, and Richard choked on his food. Amaryllis poured her father a glass of water and passed him the glass, which he reluctantly took and drank quickly. Setting his glass down, he turned to Kristina and answered her question in the vaguest way possible.

"Yes, she was happy, at least that's how she seemed to me," he replied.

"I see I am so happy to hear that. You seem like a respectable and kind man. She must have been lucky to work with you," Kristina said and put her hand on his leg. Lisa's shoulders tensed and Richard tried to move his leg away from her touch. Removing her hand and seeming to have no idea about the commotion she had caused, she casually went back to drinking her red wine.

"Tell me, Kristina, how long are you planning to stay here?" Lisa asked, eyeing her like a predator eyes her prey. Richard shot his wife a look that said 'don't start.' But his wife was adamant to hear the answer to her question and waited for the answer.

"I don't know. I am a doctor, so my schedule is very busy, but I managed to take a few weeks off work. I will try to take a few more if it means getting to know how my sister was here," she said.

The maids cleared their plates and the table whilst they went to the living room. Biscuits and tea were served to their guest. Kristina had wanted to go and excused herself, but Richard had insisted she stay and so she did. Sipping her tea slowly with her long legs crossed over one another, Kristina looked around the living room, her gaze stopping to stare in awe at the paintings on the wall.

"These paintings are so beautiful. Who's the artist?" she asked.

"Oh, we painted those ourselves as a family when I was young. They have been here for more than ten years," Amaryllis said whilst looking at her artwork proudly. They were all abstract art paintings and so many different shades and colours decorated them. They made the living room feel like an art gallery, but the big chandelier hanging in the middle of the room made the living room feel like a French castle from the olden days.

"You and your family must be very close then," Kristina said, her eyes flickering with annoyance. Amaryllis was hesitant to answer but nodded her head. There was nothing else she could say. She could not say the truth. She couldn't open her heart to a random stranger and tell her about all the family problems that they have.

Seeing his daughter's hesitation, Richard jumped in, "yes we are very close," he replied. He snaked his arm around his wife's shoulders, who tensed upon his touch. Kristina seemed to take heed of the tension in the air and decided that it was best to go.

"Well, it's time for me to go now," Kristina said as she put her teacup down on the small wooden table and stood up. They said their goodbyes and Richard showed his guest to the door.

There was a chill in the air at this time of day and the moon had already made an appearance. It was resting comfortably, high in the sky. Stars filled the majestic night sky, creating a dazzling scene. The night sky was a dark blue and, in a few hours, it would be pitch black. Regardless, it was dark, too dark for Richard to take notice of his brother's head poking out from behind the bush he was crouched down behind. James looked at the door, not daring to show his face after that night. The night where his relationship with Lisa might have been exposed. He peeked from behind the bushes to see who had opened the door. He had hoped it would be Lisa so he could call her over and explain everything to her. He would tell her that the girl was just a friend and how he loved Lisa and how he would never think about another woman whilst he was with her. Or maybe he would change that to he would never think about another woman whether she was with him or not. Yes, that sounded more romantic. He was about to leave to go to his own house when the woman that stood talking to Richard turned around, allowing him to see her face. He gasped, putting his hand over his mouth as to not make any noise and give away his hideout.

"Katerina?" he said. He knew he recognised that perfect gelled back hair and that tall lean body from somewhere. But because he was always surrounded by so many women, he thought it may have just been his mind playing tricks on him. Surely there was someone else that had similar characteristics to her. But no. This was Katerina. James could never mistake her for anyone else after he had seen her angelic face.

James watched Richard, his eyes roaming Katerina's body as she went inside a taxi. James didn't know why Lisa felt guilty for cheating on Richard. He always flirted with other women when she wasn't around. James was sure Richard was cheating on Lisa too, but Lisa would never believe whatever James had to say about Richard. After all, he was her husband and the father of her only child. Lisa trusted Richard, even if she didn't love him anymore. No matter how much it pained James to admit it, he had to admit he was jealous. Lisa never trusted James. She doubted everything he did. Whether it was something big like him choosing what hotel would be safe for them to stay at, or if it was something small like helping her choose the dishes that would be served at a party she was hosting.

James seemed to realise that his thoughts had escaped to Lisa and made himself focus again on the situation at hand. So many questions ran through James' mind. What was Katerina doing here? How did she know Richard? And the most important question of all, how did someone manage to always look so perfect?

Chapter 13

Fairies and Demons

Brushing her fingers through her hair, Amaryllis picked up her hair curler and curled her hair section by section. After she finished her hair, she let the curls fall on her shoulders. She took the plug off and put the hair curler on the heating mat. She let the hair curler cool whilst she attached her wings on her back and turned to the side, looking in the mirror to see them. Her wings had many colours of the rainbow. They were a pair of silver-lined wings with pink, green, blue, yellow, orange and purple colours filling the butterfly shape. The wings matched her colourful and creative eyeliner perfectly. Her eyeliner also looked like a rainbow with streaks of pink, green, blue, yellow, orange and purple. As she put on her sparkling silver heels, a knock on the door caused her to shift her attention to the door.

"Come in," she called, and the door was pushed open. A mop of blonde hair popped out from behind the door and Amaryllis grunted and turned her back to her uncle. He helped himself inside her room.

"Aren't you going to say a word to me? You haven't spoken to me in over a month," he said matter-of-factly.

"You are the one that came into my room. If you want to say something, then say it and leave. Also, you know exactly why I haven't spoken to you in over a month," Amaryllis turned to face her uncle. She had not looked at his face in a long time. His face had changed so much in a month. He had a light blonde beard and his eyes looked tired. Although his physical appearance might have seemed different to Amaryllis, she couldn't help but think about how from the inside, he hadn't changed at all. He was still cheating on her father. Amaryllis knew this from the heated exchanges he shared with her mother whenever he came over for dinner. She was also sure they shared more than heated exchanges when they probably met in secret.

"Look I came here to sort this thing between us. It upsets me that you won't even say a word to me when we used to spend most of our time together. We used to travel together and go on adventures together. What happened to us? We used to have so much fun and now you won't even look at me," he said, taking a deep breath. She put her hand on her hip and leaned against her desk, watching him with narrowed eyes, studying him. Then she said something neither one of them was expecting her to say.

"Leave my mother and we can go back to how we used to be," she said, still holding his gaze. Her uncle seemed to take a step back as if she had slapped him across the face. He shook his head vigorously.

"I can't. I love your mother," he said, making her laugh loudly.

"You don't love anyone. You don't love me, or my dad and you certainly don't love or have loved any woman. You just flirt with them, have sex with them and then leave them the next day," Amaryllis bit back, her voice shaking with rage.

"I love your mother and she loves me. We have loved each other for a long time. At first, we didn't act on our feelings because we thought it was wrong. But after your father started neglecting Lisa and arguing with her over the most stupid things, she came to me. Your father doesn't make her happy. He doesn't deserve her," her uncle whispered back after he slid his head out the door to see if anyone was in the hallway. Amaryllis laughed in disbelief.

"My mother is the one that fights with my father. Over everything. She doesn't just fight with my dad. She fights with everyone - the maids, the chauffeurs and me, her daughter. You are the only one that she doesn't fight with and now I know why," Amaryllis spat. Her uncle flinched as if she had slapped him. She had slapped him. Maybe not physically, but certainly verbally. James decided to leave her room, but not before shooting her an irritated look.

There was one thing she was sure of. It was that none of the fabricated lies James had come up with could change how Amaryllis saw her mother. No matter how clever or creative he might make his future lies, she knew her mother was the real villain just like him. She saw how much her mother fought with her father and how much of her rudeness and disrespect he endured. All for her, his only daughter. Sometimes she wished that he would divorce her mother. That way Amaryllis could move out with her father to a new house and there she could live in peace. In her own house, she was always the victim of most of the fights and arguments her mother initiated. Her mother couldn't seem to go a day without making everyone's life a living hell, and on top of that, she decided to cheat on her husband. No matter how much Amaryllis thought about it, her mind couldn't comprehend why her mother did what she did. She thought for hours and days and weeks for the past month, trying to come up with excuses to excuse her mother's sins. There was nothing in the world that could excuse what she did. What she did was unforgivable. Amaryllis would never forgive her for it, and neither would her dad when he finds out.

She stepped onto the enormous white boat with her glitter purse sparkling in the night. Her hair reflected the light from the moon, and it shone like the yellow sun. Her heels clicked against the boat's floor, and she heard loud music nearby. A strong gust of wind came and nearly pushed her off her balance. There was only supposed to be little wind today. She waited until the strong gust of wind went and continued her journey inside.

Looking around, her heart skipped a beat. All the tiny lights and decorations were dark coloured. Red and black dominated most of the decoration's colours. Amaryllis pulled out her phone and reread Natalie's message. She double-checked and it did indeed say that the theme of the party was fairies and sparkle. "What an odd theme name," she thought for the second time since reading the theme. The red and navy lights shining from the top of the boat warned her that the theme was anything but fairy and sparkly. The lights and decorations were so dimly lit that the light from the moon illuminated her pathway ahead much better than the lights. The ruffles on her dress jumped up and down as she made her way to the party.

The boat had two decks. The upper deck was nearly empty with only a few people that wanted to escape the loudness of the party. The lower deck was where the party was. People filled the deck; to the point where it looked like some might fall into the ocean because they were standing at the edge of the boat. Amaryllis heard the peaceful sound of the ocean waves as they hit the side of the boat. Their sound calmed down her racing heart a little, but not enough for her to stop hearing her heart ram against her chest. Her worries were proved correct when she started receiving stares as she made her way inside. The further she walked, the more people there were and the more that stared. They started pointing fingers at her wings and imitating how a fairy would fly.

"Look she thinks she's a butterfly," one boy said pointing his finger at her wings and laughing. Everybody burst out laughing and with the costumes they wore they looked like monsters. Amaryllis felt like she was in a fantasy thriller movie where she was the fairy princess and the students were the monsters that wanted to kill her. They were all dressed in scary costumes. Some had horns on their head and fake swords strapped to their hip. A few girls wore black witch hats and wore long black robes that reached to their ankles whilst holding a long broomstick. Others had all kinds of different costumes on. Some boys had vampire teeth that stuck out of their mouths and a red one-piece costume. The rest all wore different kinds of scary costumes as if it was Halloween. Most of the students had fake blood on their head or other parts of their body and many also had fake scars and wounds.

Before Amaryllis could process what had happened, something red and round came flying and hit her on the forehead. She stumbled backwards and fell on her butt. The mysterious object rolled onto the floor, revealing a red apple thrown by a real witch. Rose was dressed as a witch with a long black robe and a black hat. Her frizzy black hair helped her achieve the villainous and witchy look. Although, in Amaryllis' opinion Rose didn't need a costume. She was a real witch. Rose took this opportunity to make use of the red apple in her other hand. She screamed something that Amaryllis didn't quite catch and suddenly everyone, including Rose started throwing apples at Amaryllis. She could hear her racing heartbeat and was afraid her heart would jump out of her chest. Natalie and Isabel appeared from the crowd and rushed to Amaryllis, ducking and jumping to avoid any of the apples being thrown in Amaryllis' direction. They pulled Amaryllis inside, towards the food tables and sat down on the chairs. Some of the monsters went as far as running after them, but a strong gust of wind shut the door to the food area, blocking their entrance. A new song started playing, distracting the monsters from going after Amaryllis. They started dancing to the new song and dropped the remaining apples they were holding. It was as if they had a switch. One minute they were chasing after her and the next they were dancing.

    Once Isabel and Natalie had helped Amaryllis calm down, Isabel noticed Amaryllis' outfit. She scanned her eyes up and down her outfit. Her confused eyes seemed to grow in confusion as she spotted the sparkling bag and the sparkling wings Amaryllis had on.

    "Why are you dressed like that?" Isabel finally asked.

    "Natalie told me that the theme was fairies. I came here expecting people to be dressed as fairies but instead, I saw witches and devils," Amaryllis breathed out. Natalie bowed her head in shame.

"I asked Isabel and she told me that it was the theme," Natalie said, looking accusingly at Isabel.

"Ohh Yeah I told you that, but that's what they said in the group chat. If you guys didn't exit the group chat you would have seen that's what they said," she defended.

"The group chat became too toxic. All they talked about was Amaryllis. Derek told me about the theme a few minutes before we started getting ready. If he hadn't told me I would have been dressed as a fairy too. I should have remembered to text you. I am so sorry," Natalie said.

"It's fine, it doesn't matter. There's nothing we can do about it now," Amaryllis sniffed and wiped a tear that managed to escape. Isabel handed her a napkin hidden inside her witch robe. She wore a witch hat and carried a broomstick in her hand. She had thick black eyeliner around both her eyes and light purple contacts. Her eyes looked lifeless and monstrous. She also had fake blood on the side of her forehead and a big fake scar that showed some fake veins and other disgusting things Amaryllis could not name that could be found under the human skin. Amaryllis shuddered at the sick feeling forming in the pit of her stomach. She hated when people dressed up in scary costumes and had fake blood and fake scars on their bodies. Natalie on the other hand had red horns on her head and wore a long black sleeveless dress that had a cape attached to it. She looked like the princess of devils. Monstrous but beautiful.

There, in the distance stood Derek, watching Amaryllis with worried eyes. He signalled for Natalie to come to him, and she didn't have to be asked twice as she rushed to her twin.

"Does he seriously think you're going to believe that he's worried about you? After everything that he did? All boys are the same. They are all liars and cheaters," Isabel said. Amaryllis glanced at Isabel, watching how she looked at Derek. A month ago, she used to stare at him dreamily as if he was prince charming. Amaryllis would have never thought that Isabel would say those things about Derek, let alone take Amaryllis' side. Now, Isabel looked at Derek with angry eyes.

Natalie and Derek were still whispering whilst looking her way meanwhile Isabel complained that she was hungry and rubbed her stomach.

Isabel licked her fingers as she devoured her third burger. She had put three burgers and three fries on a big plate that looked more like a tray. Amaryllis had her hand rested under her chin and was watching her with pure fascination.

"How can you eat all of that and stay skinny?" she asked her in a voice filled with intrigue.

"It's only been three burgers and three fries. Usually, at parties I eat around five or six burgers and fries," she replied with a mouth full of fries and a burger in her hand. Isabel inspired Amaryllis to dig into her second burger. Maybe she would have luck like Isabel and wouldn't transform into a giant elephant the next day. She bit into the heavenly burger and within no time she found herself searching the burger wrap for any chicken pieces or breadcrumbs. After her frantic search was done, she realised that there was nothing left. The satisfaction she felt after she devoured her second burger was worth the two kilograms she would gain the very next day.

"Hey guys," Natalie chirped cheerfully as she threw herself on her chair and sat in-between them.

"What did he want?" Amaryllis asked, nodding her head towards Derek. He was still standing there, peering into her soul. His hands were in his pockets and his tall lean body rested against the wall. Natalie just shrugged and said that he was asking about yesterday's mathematics homework because he didn't attend the lesson yesterday. Typical.

"Please! As if we don't know what he wanted. He wants you to get him back together with Amaryllis, but that will only happen in his dreams," Isabel rolled her eyes and took a sip of her rum. Amaryllis looked at Natalie, waiting for her to tell her if what Isabel said was true but Natalie was busy flashing Isabel with her glares. That was the first time she saw Natalie lose her happy demeanour. Isabel must have noticed too because she stopped sipping her rum and looked at Natalie as if she was... scared.

Isabel gulped, "what I meant was that Amaryllis is never going to forgive him after he used her like that. He used her to get a green Lamborghini for god's sake." Natalie's glares only intensified and for a moment Amaryllis thought she didn't recognise the girl in front of her. She looked like she was about to shoot fire from her eyes at Isabel. Natalie had never lost her cool like that before. Amaryllis found herself waving her hands in front of her best friend. Natalie shook her head and readjusted her gaze on Isabel once again.

"Listen I know what he did was horrible, but if Amaryllis wants to go back to him and give him another chance, that's something only she decides. And how did you know he got a green Lamborghini?" Natalie arched her eyebrow. Isabel played with the breadcrumbs on her plate.

"I agree that Amaryllis should decide if she wants to forgive him or not, but I was just voicing what I thought would be her obvious opinion. She would never forgive him for what he did. No woman could ever forgive a man for something like that. What he did was unforgivable. He also doesn't regret anything that he did since he drove the Lamborghini to school yesterday for everyone to see what he traded Amaryllis with. He looked proud as well as if he had not done anything wrong," Isabel continued with the same spiteful tone.

"I just told you-," Natalie started saying but was cut off by Amaryllis' scream.

"Enough, stop arguing. This is my problem, not yours. Although Isabel is right. I would never forgive him for what he did. And this isn't the first time he breaks my trust. On our first date he didn't even show up and then I found out he had gone out with another girl," Amaryllis said. Vertical wrinkles started appearing on Natalie's forehead. She rubbed her forehead, but the wrinkles were still visible. She grabbed a drink and drank a bit from it before she slammed it on the table and dropped her hands to her sides. She looked too restless to move a finger.

The three girls sat there for the rest of the party, eating dessert and drinking rum. They went up to dance occasionally and tried to have as much fun as they could. They moved their bodies to the beat of the music and danced together. Sometimes they danced with random boys from their school and sometimes by themselves.

Thankfully, the party soon finished, and it was time to go home. Now they could rest from this exhausting party. More than half of the students had already rushed home. It was past their curfew, with the clock ticking past three in the morning. Natalie, Amaryllis and Isabel got up to leave. That's when Amaryllis' way was blocked by a tall figure. She looked up only to find Derek in front of her. She tried to move to the side but he mimicked her movements and every time she moved, he moved. Isabel shouted something at Derek and then huffed when he didn't answer her. Natalie nudged her harshly, making her scoff.

"I want to speak to you," he muttered in a low husky voice. Goosebumps formed on her arms, and she shuddered, feeling the morning wind hit her flesh.

"You said all you needed to say the other day. Please leave me alone," she turned to leave but he grabbed her hand, bringing her close to his chest. They stared deeply into each other's eyes and for a moment it was as if they were the only two in the world. But they weren't. There were two angry teenagers arguing right next to them, but their voices were inaudible to Amaryllis who was too captivated by her captors' gaze. The realisation didn't dawn upon her just yet but her

eyes glimpsed Natalie dragging Isabel away from them, leaving them completely alone in the boat since everybody had left by now.

Chapter 14

Poor Cinderella

Amaryllis tossed and turned in her bed. She couldn't sleep no matter how many methods she tried. She tried counting sheep but that didn't work. She tried listing random things that weren't related to each other, but that didn't work either. She had heard that listing random unrelated things could get you to sleep in under ten minutes. What a lie. She had also tried various things before these two methods, but by now she couldn't remember what she had tried. The only other method that she remembered trying was exercising. Her lower legs were still throbbing from jumping up and down, running around her room in small circles and running on the treadmill for half an hour. She had done some research on her phone and a study had shown that if she went to bed physically tired, she was going to fall asleep very fast. But the only thing that had happened was that she felt more awake than ever. She had started trying different methods a few hours ago, but she still was not asleep.

Instead, Amaryllis decided to get to the root of the problem. She wondered why she couldn't sleep. She always fell asleep as soon as her head was on her pillow. Maybe it had to do with her failing maths when she usually got top grades in the subject. She shook her head. It was much deeper than that. After thinking deeply, she discovered that the reason why she couldn't sleep was because she felt like people were taking turns to punch her and she was doing nothing to block their punches. She was standing there and taking it all.

She sat up in her bed and looked out of her terrace, the moon was full and beautiful. It shone brightly in the night sky, and she found herself going to the terrace for some fresh air. She inhaled deeply, then exhaled. She stared at the moon and the stars in the sky. The sky was full of stars tonight, which rarely happened. Usually, the sky was black and plain but tonight there was not only one treasure decorating it but many. The first treasure being the moon and the second treasure being the stars. The stars were scattered randomly across the sky. Perhaps as randomly as the random things Amaryllis tried to make her fall asleep. Near the moon, the stars surrounded the planet in almost circular patterns. Further away from the moon, some stars stood close together, like a pack or a clan. Amaryllis played with her hair, curling her straight hair into loose curls.

After staring at the sky, her mind calmed down from her racing thoughts. A big realisation dawned upon Amaryllis. She needed to defend herself against Rose and whoever else was going to try and hurt her. She needed to give Rose a taste of her own medicine. That way, Rose and any future bullies would know not to mess with her. She wondered how she could do it. She didn't know anything that she could use to hurt or humiliate Rose. Perhaps she could make her do something shameful, film her and then post it on the group chat. She wondered what she could make her do willingly, without letting her realise that it was a setup. Amaryllis thought and thought and thought but came up with nothing. Suddenly it struck her like a lightning bolt. Amaryllis had seen Rose without her Prada shoes for the first time in forever. She always wore her Prada shoes everywhere. At school, to go shopping and any other place she went to. She never left her house without them. She always shopped from Prada and other famous brands and never wore cheap and unbranded clothes. She would never wear unbranded shoes. Never. Even if it meant she had to jail herself at home until she bought another pair of Prada shoes. Since Rose was without her Prada shoes, that must only mean one thing. She couldn't afford them. Suddenly, a flashback penetrated Amaryllis' mind with the memory of her and Rose out in La Rose a couple of weeks ago. When they were out to buy desserts, Rose's card stopped working. Amaryllis had thought nothing of it until now. She thought there might have been a technical issue with the bank which is what Rose had later told her, but now Rose was wearing cheap shoes, which she would never do. That only meant one thing. Rose was broke. She didn't have enough money to buy Prada shoes anymore. Amaryllis jumped up and down in excitement. She would finally humiliate Rose. But she had to get evidence of her broke state. She knew exactly what she would do. This was a golden opportunity for Amaryllis, and she would not let this opportunity that had fallen right into her hands slip away.

She rushed inside her room and looked in the drawers of her wardrobe. She opened the first drawer and rummaged through it, but the only things she found were towels. She rummaged through the second drawer, only finding a few candles and many other random things that she had thrown in because she didn't know where else to put them. It was only until she opened the third drawer that she found her weapon. She took it out and made sure it still worked. She decided to charge it overnight, so it was ready to use the next day. She already felt confidence surging through her veins. After she was done with Rose, no one would dare to even think about hurting her. She threw herself on her comfortable bed and buried her face in her feathery pillow. Before she could even drag the covers over her body, she had fallen asleep. Snoring loudly, Amaryllis slept like a baby through the night.

The birds chirping woke her up the next day. She yawned and stretched her body across her bed, a smile stretching on her face. This was going to be a good day. This day she would remember forever. The day she took Rose down. She did her full morning routine whilst humming and dancing. She hummed whilst she brushed her teeth. She hummed whilst she changed into her school clothes, and she hummed whilst eating breakfast. Her mother and father exchanged confused glances over their daughter's sudden high spirit. It had been a while since they saw their daughter in a happy mood. After breakfast, she took her time choosing what colour lipstick she would wear. She usually wore a light pink shade. However, today was a special day. Today she needed something bold, something daring. Something that showed people that she was different. She reached for her bold red lipstick and applied it to her full lips. She also decided to leave her hair straight and not curl it. After all, she was a new Amaryllis. She didn't need her curls anymore. She would do fine without them.

Amaryllis sat crouched down with a tiny section of her head poking out from behind the dirty wall she was hiding behind. Her camera was in her hand, and she filmed the neighbourhood Rose lived in. After several takes, she finally got a good shot of Rose. Rose turned her head around and inspected her surroundings as if she was afraid someone had seen her. Amaryllis smirked; she was always paranoid. This was the only time her paranoia was rational. She filmed Rose as she walked up the steps of her house and knocked on its wooden door. When no one opened it, she sighed in annoyance and took out her keys to open the door. Rose was used to the maid opening the door for her and had not got used to opening the door by herself.

Amaryllis wondered how long Rose had lived there. She thought about how long she had pretended to still be rich. After fiddling with the key and turning the key left and right in the keyhole, Rose finally managed to unlock the door. She threw her keys in her bag and trotted inside. The camera captured the small hallway and the wooden floor of the house. Amaryllis let a low laugh escape her mouth. Rose snapped her head to the direction the sound had come from, but Amaryllis had already hidden her poking head out of sight. Amaryllis only poked her head out again when she heard the slamming of the door. She took one last photo of the house before disappearing from behind the wall. She shoved her camera inside her bag and pulled out her phone. She waited until she was out of the neighbourhood before she dialled Natalie's number and raised the phone to her ear.

"Girl you won't believe what I just caught on my camera. Rose is going to be toast after I put all these videos in our group chat. She's going to pay for everything she's done to me. After I am done with her, she's not even going to be able to show her face at school. Also, don't tell anyone else about this. The fewer people that know the better cuz I want this to be a sweet surprise to my best friend," Amaryllis said. Natalie could be heard yawning on the other side of the phone. Amaryllis furrowed her eyebrows in confusion.

"Did you just wake up? You weren't at school today, were you?" she asked.

"Yeah, I just woke up. I am not bothered to keep going to school. I have top grades in all my subjects, turning up is practically useless since all I do is file my nails and ignore whatever the teacher is blabbering on about," Natalie said.

"Lucky you, I have to pay extra attention in mathematics because I failed. Anyways, please tell me you were listening to what I said about Rose," Amaryllis pleaded.

"Of course, I heard what you said about Rose. You know you are turning into a bit of a diva," Natalie snickered through the other side of the line. Amaryllis did nothing but smile at that. A month ago, she would have argued against that, but now she would accept that comment and take it as a compliment. She had turned into a diva, but only when it required her to defend herself. She was still a good person. At least in her opinion. But what Rose and what other people had done to her in this past month had without a doubt changed her. She wasn't the sweet Amaryllis that would ignore everything others did to her anymore. No. That was all in the past. Now a new Amaryllis was born. Now she would fight back. If she didn't, then people were going to continue to mistreat her. Although she knew what she was doing was the right thing to do, she couldn't shake off this peculiar feeling that formed in the pit of her stomach.

The next day at school, Amaryllis decided to do a re-enactment of Rose's theatre performance. This was when Rose had shown the whole school Amaryllis' scrapbook that was full of photoshopped pictures of Derek and her. Amaryllis would never forget the feeling of humiliation she had felt. It was true what they said that the people closest to you were the ones that could hurt you the most because they knew all your secrets.

Amaryllis stood in the middle of the dining room, just as Rose had done a few weeks ago. To add to the effect of her performance, she decided to rent a big screen that she attached her camera to. The screen was as big as a cinema screen and so everybody would be able to see the pictures and the videos Amaryllis had taken clearly. She had a remote control in her hand to slide through the pictures and to show the next videos after a video had finished.

Thanks to her uncle, she had excellent photo-taking skills. The pictures she took of Rose and her house were very clear. She would not be able to deny that the person in the pictures was her. The pictures showed the look of disdain on Rose's face when she was in her new neighbourhood and the wooden door to her house that looked like it would fall off if someone knocked on it a bit too harshly. They also showed a glimpse of the neighbourhood Rose lived in. There was plenty of dirt and trash on the streets. The neighbouring houses had dirt on them and looked like they had been there for over a hundred years just like Rose's house.

"Attention everybody, attention. This is Amaryllis speaking. I am sure that everybody remembers me. Just a few weeks ago, the person I thought was my best friend humiliated me in front of everyone," Amaryllis said into the microphone, attracting the attention of everybody in the room. People put their plates down and left the food aisle to come and see the latest theatre performance. There had been many free theatre performances lately, to the point where the students probably had stopped going to the theatre since they could watch them for free at their school.

Students put down their forks and knives and stopped eating their food. They hurried up to where Amaryllis was standing. Derek and Natalie had just come in through the dining room door when Amaryllis had started her speech. Derek looked at Natalie with weary eyes, but Natalie just shrugged and smirked as she made her way through the crowd to Amaryllis.

"Has anyone noticed that Rose doesn't wear her Prada shoes anymore, but wears shoes that look cheap and used? Who here in this school doesn't wear branded shoes? After all, they just cost a few thousand and that's nothing anyone that goes to this school can't afford right? How shameful it would be not to be able to afford branded shoes," Amaryllis said, and students looked down at the shoes that they were wearing. They then shifted their attention to their friends' shoes. They sighed in relief when they saw that their friends had branded shoes too.

Just as Amaryllis was going to move to the fun part, she spied frizzy hair flying into the dining room. The hair was messy and looked like a lion mane, and thus could only belong to one person. Rose stood there in her cheap shoes, looking around confused as to what the commotion was about. Amaryllis had a wicked smile plastered on her face as she prepared to drop the bombshell news.

"Can you imagine not being able to afford Prada or other branded shoes? Or worse, can you imagine being poor. There is one student here who doesn't have to imagine being poor because she is poor. That student is in our year and has been going to our school for years. That student has never turned up without wearing her Prada shoes, but now she wears, and I quote 'shoes from the high street'," Amaryllis continued. Drops of sweat formed on Rose's forehead, and she lowered her bag in front of her shoes to hide them from plain sight. Amaryllis laughed wickedly as she looked at the reaction she had caused.

"I have proof of who that person is, and I have pictures and videos of the disgusting and cheap house they now live in," Amaryllis said and pressed a red round button on her remote control. Instantly, a picture of Rose's house appeared. Rose ducked her head and tried to push her way out of the dining-room door, but there were too many people gathered near the entrance. Amaryllis saw her attempt to escape and called her out.

"Rose where are you going? We are just getting to the good part. Don't you want people to see videos of your new house," she said and pressed the arrow button on the remote control to show a video of Rose fiddling with her keys and struggling to open the door to her house. Everyone concentrated their attention on Rose. Rose pushed through the crowd again, trying to exit the dining room, but was pushed back by a few students who started shouting insults at her. She started bawling her eyes out whilst Amaryllis laughed wickedly at her. Natalie joined in with Amaryllis' laughter and soon the rest of the room had joined them. Words like 'poor girl' and 'cheap' were being shouted at Rose. Rose looked like a scared cat as she looked around the room for an escape, but found none as all the students started circling her.

Nearly everybody relished in the latest scandal as they could now take out their worries and problems on Rose, who was standing there with no way out and no one to help her. It was much easier to ignore their problems and their insecurities when they could project them on someone else.

Amaryllis felt a heated glare from a pair of eyes and snapped her head up only to meet Derek's heated gaze. His eyes had a very peculiar emotion in them. Amaryllis couldn't put her finger around it, but she didn't like how it made her feel. It seemed Derek was not happy with what Amaryllis had done. She expected him to be happy. He had seen all the trouble Rose had caused for her. He had been the witness to the many wicked games she had played. However, Derek wasn't upset, Amaryllis soon realised that a very unfamiliar emotion coated his eyes. Disappointment. He was disappointed in her. Amaryllis' wicked smile fell, and a deep frown replaced it. She held Derek's gaze, trying to communicate with him using her eyes but he just stared at her with that same annoying emotion. Amaryllis felt naked under his gaze, she felt exposed. Soon guilt started to wash over her, but she shook it off. Rose deserved this. She deserved much more than this because of all that she had done to Amaryllis. She was lucky Amaryllis wasn't one to hold grudges or plan revenge. Otherwise, she would have done something much more drastic. She could have made fun of how her dad had left her mother for a twenty-year-old girl, and how Rose had not seen him since she was ten years old. Thus, she ought to be thankful that Amaryllis just wanted to give her a taste of her own medicine. Amaryllis didn't do it out of vengeance, she did it so Rose would not hurt her anymore. She expected Derek to understand. A part of her didn't care what Rose felt or what Derek thought about what she had done. Meanwhile, the other part of her felt guilty. She felt as if she had turned into a bad person whenever she stared into Derek's disappointed eyes or at Rose's tear-stained cheeks.

Chapter 15

Isabel and Rose

With rapid tears falling to the ground, one would have been surprised how they hadn't formed into pools of water already. Rose slumped down on the grass, near the school's back entrance where no one ever was around. She wailed like a baby, her shoulders shook and her body trembled. She hugged her legs tightly and rested her forehead on her knees. This was the worst day of her life. She never expected Amaryllis to do something like this. She thought she could bully and humiliate her and Amaryllis would do nothing because she could do nothing. How wrong she was. Amaryllis was capable of this and probably more.

The rustling of the leaves made her look up, and there as if she was summoned, Isabel stood next to the tree. Rose wondered when she had gotten there. She had not heard any footsteps approaching her. But this was Isabel. No one could guess anything about her or know anything about her unless she wanted you to. She could sneak up on you and you would never know. Isabel always reminded Rose of a tiger when it hides to attack its prey. The tiger takes slow quiet steps that the prey can't hear and then it attacks. Isabel was like a tiger. She could attack you and you would never see it coming. The strong negative energy radiating off Isabel made Rose aware that Isabel was looking down at her with a face full of...disappointment?

"How could you not tell me you were broke. You idiotic girl. You were always a fool," Isabel sneered. Rose flinched and her crying stopped. Isabel motioned with her hand for Rose to get up, all the while she looked away, her features coated with disgust. Rose rushed up to her feet. Stumbling, it took her a second to rebalance her feet on the ground.

"Why would I tell you? What would that change?" Rose screamed. Isabel scrunched her face up in disgust.

"I could have bought you a pair of Prada shoes, you idiot. That way no one would have suspected you being broke. You should have also been careful about who was following you to your house. How can someone follow you all the way home and you don't notice," Isabel continued her lecture. Rose shuffled on her feet and lowered her head. Tears started streaming down her cheeks like a waterfall and falling to the ground. Isabel had had enough of her meltdowns because she came and grabbed her chin and forced her head up. She glared at her with her nearly black eyes, her tight grip would no wonder leave a mark on her chin.

"Mark my words, you will not ruin anything for me. Get yourself together. What's done is done. We can't turn back time. This might even be better for us," she said. Rose squinted her eyes at Isabel in question.

"Whilst you were busy crying when Amaryllis was exposing you, instead of fighting back like you should have, I was examining Derek's reaction to what Amaryllis had done. Let's just say he wasn't pleased. He looked at Amaryllis like he didn't recognise her. I didn't even recognise her. Seems like all our games have turned her into a bad girl," Isabel continued. She let go of Rose's chin, pulled out a hair Scrunchie from her pocket and pulled her hair up into a ponytail. Isabel's eyes scanned their surroundings and she told Rose to sit down. They would now plan their next moves.

For the next couple of hours, Rose and Isabel had already had dozens of arguments about what they should do. They sat there on the grass, mapping out their devious plan to make Amaryllis' life hell and to split her from Derek. Whenever Rose suggested something, Isabel labelled it as stupid. Isabel also took all her anger out on her, screaming at her and frightening her. Rose took this opportunity to burst out into tears whilst Isabel got even angrier because she would not quiet down and she couldn't work with loud noise.

They decided to go to Isabel's house as school had nearly finished and they sneaked out the back door before anyone could see them. They walked to Isabel's house, as it was only a few minutes away and started mapping out their plans in silence as soon as they went to her room.

Her room had black walls that felt like they were closing in on the person that was inside the room. They made the room feel like a grave and Rose was shocked how Isabel could have survived one day in this room without going into depression. All the other pieces of furniture were also black. This included Isabel's bed frame, her desk and her small couch near the window. The only colourful things in her room were her pink and white makeup brushes and her colourful make-up palettes that were scattered on her black desk. If it were not for the big window that she had, that illuminated the room with sunlight, the room would have been a replica of a graveyard at night.

"And here is where I come and get close to Derek," Isabel pointed to a stickman she drew that was supposed to resemble Derek.

Rose blew at the hair falling on her face and folded her arms. Isabel looked at Rose in challenge.

"Why do you get Derek? I liked him before anyone ever did, but then Amaryllis saw him and she always gets whatever she wants. She stole him away from me. Derek was supposed to be mine. Mine, and now you want to steal him from me too," Rose complained. Isabel smacked her forehead as if Rose had just said the most stupid thing.

"How could he look at you, we have already been through this. You are ugly, you are fat. A guy like Derek would never look at a girl like you. Even the prettiest girls at our school get rejected by him again and again. If you go and pursue him, he will want to run back to Amaryllis just to get away from you," Isabel said and waved her hands frustratingly in the air.

Rose was about to say something when the sound of a baby crying distracted her. The maid came rushing in, holding a baby that looked too much like Isabel for them not to be related. The baby was a boy from all the blue he was wearing and he looked to be about one years old. He had brown hair like Isabel, but his eyes were a beautiful blue, whereas hers were nearly black. He smiled widely at Isabel, revealing a tiny front tooth. Drool started spilling from the side of his mouth and the maid tried to wipe it with a napkin, but he kept moving his head away. Isabel sprang to her feet and ushered the maid out, telling her to take him to the nanny. The maid tried to protest, but Isabel ignored her and the baby's hands that reached out for her. She slammed the door in their faces and went back to sit back on her bed.

"Is that your brother?" Rose asked, still looking at the closed door where the maid and the baby had been.

"No. He's my... cousin," Isabel said, her eyes not meeting Rose's. Even though there was no reason why Isabel would lie, Rose still doubted her answer.

Amaryllis sat on her chair, combing her hair and looking at the mirror on her dressing table. She was grateful that she had a dressing table where she could store all her make-up and hair products, and another table where she could store all her school textbooks. She thought back to what Derek had said to her after the boat party and remembered how he had later looked at her after she humiliated Rose. She wondered if he still felt the same way about her after what she did today. The repetitive question circling her mind of 'did he still love me' made her head hurt.

The comb falling out of her hand snapped her out of her daze. She bent down to retrieve her comb and continued brushing her hair, fighting all the thoughts of Derek that threatened to evade her mind. She didn't care how he felt about her. She hated him. Yes. She hated him, she told herself. The only things she would be focussing on right now were her grades and her future. She didn't have time to focus on boys. They were a waste of time and a waste of her energy. But no matter how much she tried to focus on brushing out her straight hair, she couldn't push the image of Derek and how he looked at her out of her mind. He seemed so disappointed in her. For some reason that hurt her more than when he did not show up on their first date and more than when she learnt about the bet.

Angry, she slammed her comb on her table and stormed out of her room. Maybe dinner would finally take her mind off a few things. Going down the stairs, the air smelt of pork ribs and roasted vegetables and rice. This was another one of her favourite things to eat, if she wasn't having seafood or French food.

She was wearing a pair of white ribbed shorts with a matching white ribbed t-shirt. They both had a floral pattern on them that Amaryllis loved. She had hoped that wearing something colourful that she loved would brighten up her mood. She loved anything floral and when the pattern was pink that was a bonus.

Her slippers pounded against the stairs, which alerted the trio sitting in the dining room to her presence. Amaryllis had not expected another person to be joining them for dinner, other than her uncle. She was surprised to see the beautiful woman she met the other day here. Amaryllis searched her memory for her name, but couldn't remember it. There was no use for a name since she could just call her beautiful woman. This woman was without a doubt the most beautiful woman Amaryllis had ever seen. It seemed as if her beauty increased day by day. This time she wore a red dress that showed off her long legs and had a low plunge neckline. She had on some red lipstick and her hair was once again gelled back in a sexy yet feminine way. She beamed brightly when she saw Amaryllis, which made Amaryllis look back and to both the left and right to see if she was beaming at her. She went inside and greeted the woman. Her father said that he and her mother had invited her over for dinner, though from her mother's cold expression it seemed as if it was more her father's idea.

They took their seats at the table, with Richard sitting at the head of the table and Lisa sitting next to her husband. Amaryllis sat next to her mother and Kristina sat in front of Lisa. The food was served and they all couldn't wait to taste this deliciousness. They ate their food as Kristina constantly asked Richard questions about her sister.

She sometimes asked Amaryllis a few questions too, but Amaryllis just shrugged and said a few sorrys as she didn't have an answer for Kristina. She didn't know Miss Emma very well at all.

Kristina's questions gradually became less about her sister and more about Richard. She seemed very comfortable asking him personal questions and he seemed very eager to answer them. She asked him about his hobbies, his likes, and his dislikes, as if they were on a first date getting to know each other. One would have thought Lisa's eyes would have stopped working by now, due to the number of times she rolled them at the questions Kristina asked. She also rolled her eyes whenever Kristina touched Richard on the arm. Amaryllis smirked to herself; her mother was getting a taste of her own medicine. Karma is truly beautiful especially when one does not have to move a finger to let the other person pay.

The doorbell rang for the 34554th time in the Knight home. Richard was too busy talking and laughing with Kristina to hear the doorbell ring. Lisa tried to get her husband's attention but he couldn't hear her over the loudness of his laughter. Amaryllis jumped from her seat and opened the door, knowing exactly who would be there. For once in a very long time, Amaryllis was ecstatic that her uncle had come. She welcomed him in and he smiled happily. After he stepped into the dining room, he furrowed his eyebrows at the sight in front of him. His brother was too busy laughing and talking with Katerina to notice his arrival. He still didn't understand how he knew her.

"Ah, James you came just in time. Come join us, we just started eating," Richard said. Half of Lisa's plate was empty. They hadn't just begun to eat, but of course, he would feel like that since he had not touched most of the food on his plate because he was too busy talking with Kristina. The maid rushed in and set another plate and a glass of water in front of James.

"James, let me introduce you to our new guest. This is Kristina, Kristina this is my younger brother James," Richard introduced them. Kristina looked up and for a brief moment, her smile fell. She tried to mask it by smiling again and adding extra cheerfulness to her voice, but anyone that was not in their world could have noticed her change of attitude. She stood up, extending her hand out to James. He took it and kissed her palm, just as he had done the first time when they met a few years ago. Richard shifted in his seat. Lisa stabbed her fork into her veggies, watching Richard's reaction. That was the kind of husband she had. He always liked and flirted with other women. He never paid attention to his wife. Even if men were flirting with her, he never gave out any reaction. Lisa was sure that even when he found out about her and James, he would not be jealous at all. The only thing he would care about was his image and people knowing that he was cheated on. She was also sure he was cheating on her or had cheated on her a few times at least. A women's intuition was never wrong. Lisa snapped out of her daze when she heard Richard call her.

"Are you okay honey?" he asked. Lisa nodded.

"I just got lost in my thoughts," she replied curtly. Richard turned his attention back to Kristina before Lisa had finished her sentence, making Lisa give Kristina the evil eye.

James moved his foot and nudged Lisa from under the table. He gave her a look that said 'what's wrong with you,' but she focused her attention on her food and ignored him. Richard and Kristina continued laughing and talking about random things that they found hilarious. James ate his food and with every bite, he examined Lisa's reaction to Richard and Kristina's closeness. He watched her for the rest of the dinner as she watched her husband and as her husband watched Kristina. Amaryllis leaned back in her chair and threw some popcorn in her mouth.

As soon as her uncle had come, she had finished her food quickly and asked the maid to bring her some popcorn. She had also ordered some strawberry cheesecake and asked the maid to bring it to her after half an hour. She knew she would have finished her popcorn after that time and needed another treat as she watched this cinematic masterpiece. If her mother wasn't so obsessed with what was happening, she would have thrown a fit at all the desserts she was consuming.

"Is Kristina your real name?" James asked out of the blue, putting an end to their loud laughter.

"Yes, it is," she replied, clearing her throat.

"It's just that I thought it would be something else. You don't look like a Kristina. More like a Kamilla, Katherine or Katerina," James finished, making Kristina choke on her water. Richard immediately reached for a tissue and handed it to Kristina. She took it and wiped her chest where some water had spilt. Richard shot his brother a glare, which James pretended not to see. Amaryllis looked at her uncle with confusion written all over her face. She took a few more bites of her cake and watched with fascination as the scenes of the movie unfolded in front of her. This was more like a live performance at the theatre than a movie. But as she sat there, watching them, her smile fell and her demeanour changed to a sad one. What a horrible life she had. She was relishing at the moment where her father was flirting with another woman in front of her mother and her mother's lover was sitting there, staring with jealousy at his lover's reaction to her husband, who was at the same time his brother. What a sad life her life had become. This was the only thing she could think of doing to make herself feel better. Instead of being in despair that this was her life she decided to pretend that she was happy about the drama. In reality, this only made her feel worse.

    She pushed her chair back and decided to flee to her safe place - her room. There she would gather her thoughts and rethink the kind of person she wanted to become and the kind of person she was becoming. Whereas feelings of happiness and kindness used to fill her daily, lately feelings of vengeance and hatred filled her. Amaryllis felt like a completely different person. She felt like she didn't recognise herself. In the past month, she had changed drastically and not for the better. She used to have top grades in all her subjects, and she used to treat people with kindness, even the ones that had wronged her. Now she was failing maths and God knows what other subjects she would fail when she took more tests. She now also enjoyed the suffering of someone that had wronged her. That was the worst change Amaryllis could think of so far. If her physical appearance would have changed as much as her insides, she would not be recognisable, even to her parents.

Chapter 16

Lying Cheater

Richard buttoned up his white shirt and was getting ready for his meeting. He was wearing his plain black trousers he always wore to work and his patent black shoes. Around his fat wrist, there was a silver watch and around his chubby finger, his gold wedding band sat. The same gold wedding band that was around Lisa's finger.

Lisa was sleeping soundly in their bed, her blonde hair sprawled out on her pillow. She wore her favourite nightgown. It was a red silk mini dress with a lace hemline. She looked like an innocent angel while she was asleep, but Richard knew her to be the opposite. Richard knew she was a devil in disguise. She was a horrible woman and soon she would meet her doom. Richard had always had his suspicions about his wife cheating on him. But he never once imagined that she would have the audacity to cheat on him with his brother. His suspicions had been there ever since he became engaged to Lisa. On the night of their engagement party, Lisa had confessed to him that she used to date James. He found out that James was the person she could not forget. He was the reason why she had turned Richard down so many times. He was the reason why Richard's friends made fun of him for being rejected so many times by the same woman. Richard's blood boiled and he felt like his soul had been set on fire. In front of James and Lisa, he pretended to be ignorant of their sins and never revealed how he truly felt whenever his brother came to visit them. He never revealed that he felt like strangling James until all the air run out of his lungs, whenever James looked towards Lisa or spoke a word to her, even if it was a simple hello.

Not until a few years ago, did his suspicion levels rise when he noticed the flirtatious side glances they gave to one another. He thought perhaps that he was imagining things. Maybe he had finally gone mad. Surely if something was going on others would notice, like the maids or even his daughter. They would then tell him what had been happening behind his back. If any of them knew what was happening and did not tell him, they would be equally as guilty. He tried to ignore the warning signs but he just couldn't do that any longer.

Then that day came. The day all his suspicions were confirmed. The day he went to visit that hotel for his work. The day he found his wife's bag sprawled on the floor of a hotel room. He had picked the bag up and rummaged through it, not believing his eyes. But then he saw a photo of baby Amaryllis. She was smiling in the photo and it showed her front tooth. She was about a year old and some of her teeth had already come out. That photo confirmed it was his wife's bag. One of the hotel staff he asked informed him that the woman had come with a young man. The hotel staff member informed him that the man looked to be in his late twenties with blonde hair and blue eyes. Richard had no suspicions or doubts left. He was now sure of his wife's infidelity. He just did not comprehend how stupid and careless they were. They went to a hotel in broad daylight and booked a room. Richard wondered how they weren't afraid someone they knew would see them. Maybe they didn't care. But Richard would certainly make sure they do.

He was flabbergasted that his brother whom he also considered his son had stabbed him in the back. He had put him in the best schools and made sure he had the best life after their parents died. He had given him everything anyone could ever want - expensive cars, money and most important of all, family.

He felt something press against his hand and that bought him back to the present moment. He looked down only to find his hand was tangled in the knot he was trying to make with his tie. He fiddled with his tie and started dragging it off to free his hand. Struggling to free his hand, he yanked it off harshly and threw it on the floor. He breathed heavily as if he was a dragon that was getting ready to breathe fire at his foe.

Staring at his wife, he moved closer to her bedside. He knelt over and grabbed some of her hair, making her shift in her sleep. He made a fistful and leaned closer so his mouth was right next to her ear.

"I know what you did at the hotel," he whispered, but Lisa just shifted more in her bed and tried to turn around. Letting go of her hair, he grabbed a pair of keys from one of his top drawers on his nightstand. Inside his black wardrobe, at the bottom, there was a black storage box with a silver keyhole. He unlocked it and threw the tiny door open. Reaching inside, he pulled out a gun. He filled it with bullets and locked the box.

Anxiety and stress filled the air around every inch of the school. It was nearly exam season, also called stress season, but mostly by students. Despite it being exam season, it seemed as if the students could not stay away from drama. People rushed from their classrooms and towards the female bathrooms. Some teachers could be heard shouting at their students to sit down and not leave whilst other teachers had rushed out with their students.

There, outside the female bathrooms, laid Rose unconscious on the floor. An ambulance had arrived within minutes and paramedics carried a stretcher inside the school. Rose was lifted onto the stretcher and her hands flopped to the side, making her look like she was dead. The school nurse assured everybody that she had fainted from stress and that it was nothing severe. Students stood frozen to the ground as they watched the poor girl of the school be taken to the hospital. Thank the lord there was free healthcare in England. Amaryllis gasped as she watched the result of her recent actions. Derek watched Amaryllis and shook his head in disappointment. Amaryllis saw his reaction and took long strides towards him. As soon as she was near him, they moved away from everyone and went into an empty classroom.

"What the hell is your problem with me? Why are you looking at me as if I have killed someone?" she asked as she shut the door behind her.

"Look at what you have done to Rose. She's in the hospital because of what you did. You know how sensitive she is and you still went and did what you did," he said harshly. Amaryllis rolled her eyes. As if she knew this would happen. Rose had humiliated her so many times yet she had not gone and fainted in front of the entire school. Rose was such a drama queen.

"Don't you remember what she did to me. Look at me, I picked myself up piece by piece without anyone's help. She could have done the same thing instead of putting on a show for the whole school to see. Also, this is the first and last time I say this but I only did what I did to protect myself from her, she left me no other choice," she nearly screamed.

"That's a lie and you know it. You could have told the headteacher and she would have put an end to her bullying. The only thing good about Mrs Smith is that she doesn't tolerate bullying. She would have expelled her immediately if you told her what she had done. But I know why you didn't tell Mrs Smith, it's because you wanted to get revenge," he said, sounding harsher with each word he uttered. Amaryllis stomped her foot on the floor and threw her hands up in the air in exasperation.

"Stop it, just stop talking to me. Stop looking at me and judging me. I can do whatever I want. And yes, maybe you are right, maybe I did want revenge and you know what, she deserved so much more. I was very merciful in what I did compared to all the things that she had done to me," she screamed. The door was opened. For once it wasn't thrown open and in came Isabel and Natalie.

"Hey guys," Natalie greeted cheerfully, not reading the atmosphere of the room. Or maybe she did but didn't care. Isabel did the thing she always did when she saw Derek, at least when Amaryllis and Natalie weren't there. She flipped her brown curls backwards and mastered a flirtatious smile as she batted her long eyelashes at him. Amaryllis noticed Isabel's flirtatious side make a return and stormed out of the room. Natalie followed behind her as Isabel turned her full attention to Derek.

"Did you see what happened to poor Rose?" Isabel said. Derek nodded sadly.

"It's so sad and she doesn't have anyone to defend her or stand by her. No one at all. At least Amaryllis had you and Natalie. But Rose will be fine, don't worry," Isabel said as she rubbed Derek's arm up and down, making his tense muscles relax.

"I just did not expect that from Amaryllis. Especially since she's the only one apart from me that knows that Rose takes medication for her anxiety," Isabel added when Derek said nothing. Derek's head snapped up at Isabel's words.

"She takes medication?" he muttered more to himself. Isabel nodded, a sad expression filling her face, although the wicked twinkle in her eyes revealed her true feelings about the matter.

"I saw you with her the other day after Amaryllis...told everyone she was poor," he said, changing the subject and struggling to find the appropriate words to describe what Amaryllis had done.

"Yes, I was trying to comfort her. I mean I don't like her but I felt sorry for her after what Amaryllis did," Isabel said, quickly covering up the truth and putting her hand on her heart as if what had happened to Rose had pained her.

Derek sighed and ran his hands through his messy hair. Isabel lost her sad facade and watched him dreamily. Derek was too busy in his world filled with disappointment in Amaryllis to notice Isabel's facade slip away. To say that he was disappointed would be the understatement of the century. He always thought Amaryllis was kind and had a heart of gold. That's why she won his heart. He thought all girls were the same until he met her, but now she was becoming like the rest of them. She was becoming selfish and cruel.

"You seem very upset. Do you want to go and have a drink?" Isabel said kindly.

Kristina's mouth twitched up into a smile for the most boring thing Richard said, but her eyes didn't mimic her mouth. Her eyes were filled with an emotion that could only be described as hate.

It wasn't hard for Kristina to put on a fake smile since that's what she did whenever one of her patients that she didn't like came for a visit at her clinic. That was all the time since she hated all of her patients.

Amaryllis waved her hands in front of Kristina's face, regaining her lost attention and unknowingly helping her refocus her attention on her current problem. Richard and his little family. She watched as he interacted with each of his family members. His brother, his wife and his daughter. She even watched how he interacted with some of the younger maids. For a man like Richard, she wouldn't have been surprised if he had a relationship with one of the maids. He was definitely the type of man to go for girls that were half his age. But he treated the maids respectfully like one would treat someone working for them. It seemed he had a very professional relationship with them.

They were all sitting in the living room, talking and eating some chocolate chip cookies Amaryllis had made. Kristina watched as Amaryllis went around and offered cookies to everyone. Richard took a few and kissed his daughter on the cheek. His smile wasn't stretched across his face, but his smile reached his eyes and his eyes lit up whenever he spoke to his daughter. Kristina smirked.

"So, his daughter is his weakness," she thought. Amaryllis offered cookies to her mother and her uncle, but they did not take any and were mostly silent throughout their time in the living room. Kristina noticed how Richard looked at his wife, Lisa. He looked at her how she looked at him, with hatred. Richard also looked at his brother in a very similar way. She felt the tension between them the first time James came to visit. Although, that didn't matter to her. The important thing to her was that she found out who was dear to Richard. That was clearly his daughter. Kristina noticed that Amaryllis loved her dad very much and that she seemed very close to him. Whenever she told a story or spoke about something, it was about something she did with her father. Never her mother or her uncle. Kristina took notice of Lisa's sudden change of style. Lisa wore a tight dress that hugged her body in all the right places and wore her blonde hair gelled back just like Kristina did. The first two times she had seen Lisa, she always had her hair up in a bun and the dresses she wore were always loose. Kristina also noticed Richard's change in style, today he wore blue ripped jeans and a black t-shirt. Whereas, for the past month he had always worn black trousers, whether he was going to work or not, and he also always wore long sleeved white or blue shirts. At least that's what he always seemed to be wearing in the pictures her spies had taken of him every week for the past month. The only person apart from Amaryllis, who had not had a change of style since Kristina last saw him was James. He always wore blue jeans and a t-shirt or a hoodie. Right now, he was wearing blue jeans and a white hoodie that had a few leaves on it. Kristina guessed the leaves probably came from the forests he visited all the time to take photographs for his work.

    "Well, I think it's time for me to go now. Thank you so much for this lovely evening and for the cookies. They were delicious," Kristina said looking at Lisa, James, and Richard, and then at Amaryllis. She smiled at them and gave Amaryllis an especially huge smile, which she returned excitedly. Amaryllis didn't know this, but Kristina would slowly lure her in. She would spend much time with her, make Amaryllis like her even more than she currently did and make her trust her. Then she would strike.

"Why do you want to go? You just came. Please stay longer. We really enjoy your company, don't we dad?" Amaryllis begged Kristina then looked at her father for support. It seemed Kristina's mission of making Amaryllis like her and trust her would not be too hard.

"Of course, we do, but if Kristina wants to go then we shouldn't pressure her," he said. Kristina smiled in gratitude. Amaryllis breathed in and out angrily.

"If your father doesn't mind, you and I can have coffee or whatever you teenagers like to drink these days and I can tell you more about my adventures in Sweden in the winter," she said. Amaryllis' face lit up like a light bulb and she jumped up and down clapping her hands. She looked at her father who nodded in permission, meanwhile, Lisa scoffed, giving Kristina a dirty look. The maid handed Kristina her coat and she threw it on and belted it up. Pulling her hair out from under the coat, she pushed it behind her shoulders. Her coat was a dark navy colour, an almost black coat. She wore nude tights and black court shoes. Her dark colours matched the colour of her soul perfectly. Kristina made her way to her car as Amaryllis and Richard waved her goodbye from the door. The moon only managed to brighten the gloomy night sky a little bit as the clouds battled with the moon and covered it with their smoke. The night was as silent as death and the wind was non-existent. The leaves on the trees barely moved. It was as if everything was dead. Kristina walked elegantly to her car, seemingly unbothered by the downpour of rain. The rain cascaded down her head and her shoulders and onto her clothes. Her body made the water turn into an elegant waterfall. She passed through a few rose bushes that had the most beautiful roses. At night it was hard to tell their colours but the bushes were filled with a variety of colours. They were filled with pink, orange, white and yellow roses. Kristina unlocked her car door and helped herself inside.

She slammed the door when she saw Richard and Amaryllis had gone inside and took a deep breath.

"Emma why were you so stupid?" she whispered, still gazing at the door where Richard had stood a second ago. The door which was white and had a pink door handle was now closed. To think that only a pretty little door separated Kristina from her enemy. Kristina's phone rang, interrupting her angry thoughts. She pulled it out from her coat and answered the call.

"What do you want? I told you I am not coming back anytime soon. Just get another doctor to fill my place and don't call me again. When I decide to come back, I will call you," she said. She rolled her eyes at the disapproving tone that came from the other end of the line. She opened her mouth to speak but the person ended the call. She pulled the phone back and stared at it in shock. She dialled the number back, but it went straight to voicemail. She put a fist in her mouth to avoid screaming.

Swallowing two paracetamol tablets, she hoped they would relieve the astounding headache that had developed as soon as she stepped foot into Richard's house. She hoped she would have better luck this time, although, for the last month of her being here, no painkiller seemed to be able to rid her of any of the horrible headaches she got.

She massaged the back of her neck, hoping to relieve some of the stress she felt and took one last look at Richard's house.

"You will pay for what you did Richard Knight. You will pay for everything. You will suffer the same loss I suffered. I will show you what it feels like to lose a part of your soul just like you made me feel dead whilst I was still alive," she sneered and started her car. She pressed on the gas pedal and turned her steering wheel vigorously, speeding out of the evil king's castle faster than a race car driving in a race.

Chapter 17

You're Disgusting

Natalie and Amaryllis spent their Saturday in their usual way. They went shopping, ate lunch at a French restaurant, went shopping again at a different mall and were now going to Starbucks for some much-needed coffee.

With dozens of bags in both their hands, their heels clicked as they made their way to Starbucks. Amaryllis' body swayed from side to side as the heavyweight of the bags kept her body unbalanced against the ground. They carried bags from many different shops, but the most noticeable shop whose name was plastered on most of the shopping bags was Zara. Whenever Amaryllis was feeling down, she shopped at Zara and it instantly brought her mood up.

From the corner of her eye, she thought she spotted someone that looked like Derek and Isabel, sitting across from each other at a table in the outdoor seating area of Starbucks. She shook her head at her absurdness and continued to the Starbucks entrance door. Derek never gave Isabel any attention although she had practically begged him for it. That was in the past though. Isabel was now her friend and she would be breaking girl code if she went out with her friend's ex-boyfriend.

Suddenly, she heard someone laugh and at that moment she knew she wasn't mistaken. That was definitely Isabel's laugh. Without a doubt. She turned her head around, almost in slow motion, petrified to witness her fears become reality. There, sitting on a table not too far from the entrance door, were Derek and Isabel. Derek seemed to be talking whilst Isabel laughed at everything he said. If Amaryllis wasn't tired from all the shopping she had done, she would have thought that Isabel laughed even before he started his next sentence. Isabel always found an opportunity to physically touch Derek. In the few seconds, Amaryllis had examined them, Isabel had touched his arm twice and pretended to pick something from his hair. She probably wanted to run her fingers through his soft hair. She also saw Derek put his hand over Isabel's and smile warmly at her. She felt her heart drop to her stomach. Someone breathed loudly next to her and she heard something drop to the ground. Natalie crouched down and breathed heavily whilst her bags rested on the ground.

"I can't carry these anymore. What was I thinking buying all these things," Natalie complained, but Amaryllis didn't hear anything she said. Natalie looked up at Amaryllis' face and followed where her eyes were set, only to find her brother and her friend out together. She shrieked loudly, attracting the attention of customers on the other tables, and the attention of Derek. He sprinted up to his sister.

"What's wrong? Are you okay?" he asked her as his eyes looked worriedly into hers. Her eyes had a look of betrayal.

"Am I okay? What a stupid question. How dare you do this to Amaryllis. This is the third time you have hurt her. Don't come to me for help anymore because there's nothing I can do after what I just saw," she said and picked up her bags one by one. It took a foot being tapped harshly against the ground for Derek to realise that Amaryllis was standing next to Natalie and he turned to her.

"Amaryllis we were just having coffee, there's nothing between us I swear," Derek said. Isabel slammed her coffee cup on the table and marched up to the lovebirds.

"Why do you explain yourself to her? Can't you see she doesn't want you? She's not even your type," Isabel spat. Derek shot Isabel a menacing look and wrapped his hand around Amaryllis' arm. He dragged her away from Isabel despite her protests. She freed her arm from his hold as soon as she could set her bags down.

"I thought you changed and didn't have all of that hatred and jealousy in your system, but I was wrong," Amaryllis said, looking in Isabel's direction.

"Please, me jealous? You think everybody is jealous of you because you think you are the prettiest and the smartest girl in the school, and that all the guys want you," Isabel spat. Natalie stood there, horizontal wrinkles appearing on her forehead, completely taken aback by the true face of Isabel she saw for the very first time. Natalie had always defended Isabel and said that Amaryllis misunderstood her. Now she saw her true colours. All this time she was after Derek. At the boat party, she kept repeating that Amaryllis wouldn't forgive Derek and she seemed so adamant about it. Now Natalie understood it was because she wanted Derek for herself. Now it all made sense to Natalie. What Natalie failed to understand was why she pretended to be Amaryllis' friend when she despised her.

It would not take long for Natalie to figure out why Isabel did this. Natalie was very intelligent and one of her best qualities was that she was a fast thinker and a great problem solver. Natalie started putting her great problem-solving skills to the most important life problem she had yet encountered.

"I mean your words just spoke volumes. It revealed your deep jealousy and hatred. I just don't understand why you pretended to like me and be my friend?" Amaryllis questioned. Natalie seemed to scrutinise Isabel. She seemed to be deep in thought and decided to explode and share the conclusions that she had reached.

"I know why," she exclaimed, making all three turn their heads in her direction. Derek ran his hand down his face. He knew it wouldn't take long for his genius sister to figure everything out.

"She planned to get close to Amaryllis and convince her not to forgive Derek," Natalie explained simply. Derek looked between Natalie and Isabel as he comprehended what Natalie said. Amaryllis wasted no time letting out her anger and frustration as she used her bags to hit Isabel in the face. Derek tried to step in-between them to intervene, but Natalie jumped forward, making him stumble backwards. Natalie smacked Isabel with her bags as well. Isabel shrieked as she was forced to take multiple steps backwards. She screamed as she tried to flee and more bags hit her. Amaryllis and Natalie shouted insults at her as she sprinted away from them, nearly falling to the ground as she tripped on a stone. She picked up her purse from the table and disappeared.

Natalie and Amaryllis gave each other a high-five as Derek looked at them, looking horrified. He always knew girls fought, but he just thought they pulled each other's hair or clothes. He never imagined they attacked each other with more than twenty shopping bags. They shrugged at him and went inside Starbucks for a coffee as if nothing had happened because nothing and nobody could ruin their weekend plans.

After her eventful afternoon, Amaryllis returned home for a quiet evening. But a quiet evening, she would surely not get. All the clothes she had bought were sprawled on her bedroom floor. A dozen of mini dresses could be spotted in varieties of colours like purple, pink, red and blue. There were also many different types and styles of top wear. Some tops were cropped, some were strapless, some were sleeveless and some had long sleeves. A few miniskirts could also be spotted. Some were hidden underneath other clothes, with only a tiny section of them peeking out. Others were on top of other dresses and top wear, and some were on her bed. All the skirts on her bed had beautiful pearl embellishments that made them fit for display at a fashion house. Those were in no doubt her favourite.

Although Amaryllis would usually feel better after going on a shopping spree, for some reason she still felt sad and anxious. Not even Zara with all of their beautiful and colourful pieces could help lift her mood this time.

The pile of clothes stood in front of her closet as she picked one piece of clothing up at a time. Hanging them on the white wooden hangers, she put all the tops in the middle double doors in her wardrobe and all the dresses in the doors next to them.

A knock on her door stopped her hanging activity. She felt her heart beat faster. She wished it was her dad because she had experienced enough drama for one day. Alas, her wish did not come true and in entered Lisa, her beloved mother. Lisa smiled, her signature fake smile stretching across her face. She examined the clothes still in the pile and smiled excitedly for the first time in a long time. Amaryllis shot her a confused look. Her mother never showed any genuine emotions, except for when they were negative.

"Darling let me help you. Oh, these pieces are all so beautiful. This dress is the latest and hottest trend," Lisa said, picking up a white mini dress. Amaryllis huffed loudly, making Lisa arch her eyebrow. Lisa's mood soured and the mother Amaryllis was used to made a return.

"What's wrong darling?" she said, attempting to touch Amaryllis, but she inched away from her mother and inched closer to her wardrobe. She put another fashion piece in her wardrobe. This piece was a white dress embellished in pearls. Pearls and white were trending and so most of the pieces Amaryllis had bought in the past few months were white and had pearls.

"Amaryllis I am talking to you," her mother dropped the piece she was holding on the floor and looked sternly at her daughter. Amaryllis knew that if she didn't say anything, her mother would only get angrier. She knew if she lied, her mother would know, so she decided to tell her the truth.

"I saw Derek with Isabel today. They were out at Starbucks and they looked like they were out on a date," she said. Her mother grumbled something and put her hands on her hips. Amaryllis had told her mother she had dated Derek and that they split because he lied to her. She didn't tell her about the bet as she wasn't that close to her mother and she thought she would have blamed her for it somehow. Amaryllis also told her he had wanted to get back together with her but she had refused.

"All men are the same. They all cheat and lie. Don't get upset darling, you will find someone better," Lisa said. Amaryllis felt the blood rushing through her veins. She felt it boil and burst in flames as her face turned red. She could not believe her mother was talking about unfaithfulness when she was cheating on her father with his brother. Amaryllis could not hold it in any longer and let all the secrets and emotions she had kept locked in, out.

"You can't talk about cheating when you are cheating on my dad," Amaryllis screamed. Her mother took a step back and instinctively put her hand on her chest. She opened her mouth and started to move it but the words were not coming out.

"What? You have nothing to say?" Amaryllis said. For the first time in her life, she was speaking to her mother without stuttering or any fear and all her mother could do was shut up and listen to her daughter.

"You have done nothing but argue with me all my life and look at everything I do as deserving of a lecture. But have you looked at yourself? You are disgusting!" she said and her mother's face turned so pale it would have been hard to distinguish her face from snow if snow had been falling from the sky at this exact moment.

"And don't you deny it because I have seen you together in this very house. Remember the time you gave me a lecture about getting detention and fighting with another student? That was the day I witnessed your infidelity. That was the day I found out my mother was a-," she stopped herself as she couldn't bring herself to say the word. Her mother had grabbed her chair from her desk and had taken a seat on it. Lisa put her face in her hands whilst Amaryllis tried to calm her fuming heart. She continued putting all her clothes on the hangers as her mother silently wept. Amaryllis would have thought she felt like crying but she didn't. She had cried many times before and now she felt as if all the tears were drained from her body. She felt as if she had no tears left to shed and her heart felt like it was beating, but not alive.

Her heart felt like it had turned to stone when she had spoken about her mother's infidelity out loud. A part of her was hoping it would not be true and so she avoided telling anyone about it because she was hoping that if she didn't say it out loud then it wouldn't be true. When she said it out loud, it felt so real and it tore her apart from the inside. She put the last piece inside her wardrobe and closed the door. Her mother had finished her weeping and was sniffing silently.

Lisa wiped her tears with the sleeve of her lilac dress and faced her daughter. She held her head up high and stared at her daughter. She seemed to stare right into Amaryllis' soul and the wall she had put up for years seemed to have dismantled. She decided to show Amaryllis how she felt.

"Since we are being honest, I have something too that I need you to know," Lisa said. Amaryllis' fingers were tangled in one another as her hands rested comfortably below her stomach.

"I have indeed been cheating on your father with his brother, but what you don't know is that your uncle used to date before I married your father," she said. Amaryllis looked at her as if she was waiting for her to finish what she wanted to say. She soon realised that her mother had nothing else to say.

"That does not change anything. You are still married to my dad and you cheated on him," Amaryllis said through clenched teeth.

"That is true, but what I mean is that I didn't cheat with my husband's brother, I cheated with my ex-boyfriend," she said. Amaryllis looked at her like it was hard for her to comprehend what she was saying. Her mother had no doubt turned stupid. What she was saying made no sense.

"No, you did cheat with your husband's brother. I don't care if he was your ex-boyfriend before," Amaryllis corrected her mother, making her mother scrunch up her face in annoyance. Amaryllis picked up her shopping bags one by one and put them all inside one another. She wanted to leave her room but her mother blocked her way. Amaryllis threw the bags on the floor and put her hands on her hips.

"You have always treated me like I am the bad guy and that's because you think your father is an angel," her mother said. Amaryllis looked at her mother, mastering her emotionless facial expression.

"Your father always flirts with other women in front of me and in front of everybody, but no one says anything. Of course, because he is a man. If I flirted openly with men, I would be called a whore," she said, her eyebrows lowered and pulled closer together. Amaryllis looked at her mother with pure contempt. So, this was how she was planning to excuse her behaviours, by making things up about her dad? Amaryllis knew there was no point in denying or challenging what her mother had accused her dad of. Instead, she decided to pretend to accept what her mother had said.

"So what? Are you seriously comparing him flirting with women to you kissing and probably sleeping with his brother," Amaryllis bit back. Her mother looked like she had to master all the patience in the world not to scream. Her face had started to turn red from rage and she clenched her hands into fists. Her fingernails most likely dug into her skin and would leave a mark, and her knuckles turned white. She bit her lip, looking as if she was preventing herself from screaming. This was the first time she had seen her mother holding herself back. Usually, she would scream and let everything she wanted to say out. For a second, Amaryllis was worried something would happen to her mother. That perhaps she might explode.

"I am saying your father is not innocent. He's the reason our relationship is broken. He barely pays any attention to me. He pays more attention to the women that come to our party half-dressed than to his wife," her mother said. Amaryllis shook her head. None of what her mother said was true. Her father was kind, caring and faithful. It was true he was always nice to the women at the parties, but he was respectful and he was being friendly. He treated them exactly like he treated the men at the parties - with respect. He wasn't flirting. Her mother was trying to blame her dad for her infidelity to make herself feel better. But even if her father didn't pay attention to her and he did flirt with women, she could have asked for a divorce. She could have spoken to him and communicated her concerns. Instead, she went and cheated on him. What her mother had done was unforgivable and she knew that.

"Deep down you know you made a mistake. You can't blame dad for anything. You could have divorced him but you decided to become a cheater," Amaryllis said, feeling exhausted. This is why she never told her mother about any of her problems. Her mother always blamed her for everything. That was her superpower. Blame. The only person she didn't blame when things went wrong was herself.

"You think I don't feel guilty? I know what I did was wrong, but I am telling you your father has been flirting with other women. He cheated on me first. That's why I cheated because I felt disrespected, ignored and unloved," she said. Amaryllis threw herself on her bed. Her hair sprawled on the bedsheets and her legs hung over the bed. She took her pillow from the side and hugged it tightly.

"Mum, we are just going in circles right now. I am really tired and don't want to talk about it anymore," Amaryllis said and shifted on her bed to lay down on her other pillow. Her mother turned to leave. Just as she pushed the door handle down, black shoes walked away from behind the door without making a single sound. Lisa took one last look at her daughter before she left her room. This was the first time their conversation had ended with Lisa not having the last word. Lisa walked in the opposite direction the shoes had gone in and towards her bedroom.

Chapter 18

Derek is Mine

Slamming the door shut, Isabel went into her room. She snatched her closet door open and took out a black hoodie. She tore it apart with her hands and with the help of scissors she found on the floor. Her eyes swam with tears and she sniffed, her tiny nose turning red.

The clicking of heels alerted Isabel that she was not alone. She kept her attention on the hoodie and kept tearing it apart as Rose came to a stop in front of her.

"What are you doing? Is that Derek's hoodie?" Rose asked, trying to reach for the hoodie. Isabel threw her prized possession across her room and then threw the scissors against the wall. She tossed herself on her bed.

"Go away, leave me alone," Isabel mumbled as she curled up into a ball. Rose didn't need to be asked twice as she left her room. Isabel's body rocked as strangled sobs left her body. Small but heavy footsteps approached her bed. The small creature climbed on her bed and laid next to her. He used his chubby and small fingers to wipe away her tears as he snuggled up to her chest.

"Mummy why you sad?" he mumbled, snuggling deeper into her chest. Isabel stopped her crying and hugged her little son to her chest. She rubbed her hands up and down his tiny back as his eyes fluttered shut. After a few more back rubs, his snoring alerted her that he had fallen asleep. She left him on the bed and put a blanket over his body.

Planting a kiss on his forehead, she took one last look at her son before picking up the remainders of the hoodie. She tossed them in the bin and took the scissors and hid it in the drawer. Opening the last drawer with a key, she took out a huge piece of paper that had 'B' written at the top of the page, in bold red.

"If you won't be mine then no one else can have you," she said. Reaching into the drawer again she pulled out a gun, a wicked grin etching across her face. She manoeuvred around, taking one last peek at her son. He was still snoring loudly. It pained her that she would not see him again, but she had no other choice. She knew he would be fine with her mother. She always took good care of him as if he was her son.

Concealing her gun under her clothes, she rushed down the stairs and past her house door, ignoring her mother's calls. She stole the keys from the driver and jumped in her car. Taking the plan out of her pocket, her eyes scanned through it.

"I did wish I wouldn't have to do this, but Derek, you left me no other choice," she muttered and scrunched up the plan, throwing it to the back seats. She started her car and pressed the gas pedal. Speeding out of her driveway, she nearly ran over one of the maids. The poor maid stumbled and fell backwards, dropping the basket of fruits she was carrying. Isabel rushed out through the gate, ignoring her mother's worried pleas.

Isabel continued with the same speed until she pulled into Amaryllis' house. She parked diagonally in their driveway and pulled out the gun she hid in her clothes. Specifically in the pocket located inside her jacket. She had no experience with guns. She fiddled with the gun for a moment and then decided to place it securely at the back of her jeans. Her fists pounded on the door until a maid opened it. The maid recognised her as Amaryllis' friend and invited her in.

The last time she was here she thought she could be friends with Amaryllis. She was a nice and fun person to be around. However, deep down Isabel knew they would always be enemies. Derek made sure of that every time he ran after Amaryllis. If only he didn't love Amaryllis. If only he loved her. But he did not love her. He did not even see her. He only had eyes for Amaryllis.

Isabel was now standing in front of Amaryllis' door. She took a deep breath. There was no going back now. She had to do what she had to do. She went inside her room and heard the shower running. She decided to wait patiently on her bed.

After thirty minutes, Amaryllis came out with her hair soaking wet, wearing a pair of white joggers and a tank top. As soon as she saw Isabel, her eyes nearly bulged out of their sockets as if she had seen a ghost. As if sensing danger she walked over to her carefully, but stopped a few metres away from her.

"What are you doing here?" she asked calmly, but Isabel could tell from her tight jaw that she was anything but calm.

"I came here to tell you to stay away from Derek. He's mine," Isabel said curtly. Amaryllis snickered and covered her mouth with her hand so no sound escaped but it was too late. Isabel's nostrils flared up.

"Yours? He doesn't even see you," Amaryllis said, emphasising the see. Isabel's chest heaved up and down as she closed her eyes and tried to calm the firing rage building inside her.

"I am asking you to leave him alone. Otherwise, you leave me no choice," Isabel warned, coming up from the bed and walking to Amaryllis so they were only a few feet apart.

"You are crazy if you think that I am running after him, he's the one running after me. But I will never forgive him if that's what you are worried about. Because I have something called self-respect, I won't ever forgive anyone that has wronged me in such a way," Amaryllis finished. Isabel huffed angrily as she stomped her foot on the ground.

"Don't lie to me. I know it's you who always talks to him, and whenever I see him, you are always around him," Isabel said, her hands starting to shake. Amaryllis began to look at Isabel peculiarly. She examined her from head to toe and then used her phone to start dialling a number, but Isabel grabbed the phone from her hand and threw it behind her on the bed.

"Ok listen, calm down. I just think I should take you to the hospital because you don't seem okay," Amaryllis said whilst putting her hands up in front of her. Isabel shook her head.

"I am fine. It's you who's not going to be fine because you won't even make it to the hospital," Isabel said as she pulled her gun from her jeans and aimed it at Amaryllis. Amaryllis screamed in shock.

"You can say your last words now, or don't," Isabel said as she started pulling the trigger. Without thinking, Amaryllis did the only thing she could do. She turned on her heel and sprinted out of her room. Isabel fired a shot but missed as it hit the door. Amaryllis screamed for help as she sprinted down the stairs. The maids came rushing as they heard her pleas to call the police.

"What's happening Miss Knight?" a maid asked as she rushed towards the bottom of the stairs. She gasped as she saw Isabel with a gun and immediately rushed to the living room and picked up the home telephone. She started dialling the police number whilst Amaryllis jumped off the last few stairsteps and landed on the ground. She screamed in pain and clutched her ankle. Hopping on her good leg, she made it to the door. Isabel followed after her, but not before shooting the maid that was trying without a doubt to call the police. The maid screamed in pain as she clutched her bloody stomach. She passed out on the floor, the phone falling from her hand and rolling down the floor until it stopped at the sofa leg. Isabel continued her journey through the door and fired a couple of shots, but still missed as Amaryllis continued ducking and swaying from side to side to save her life.

A blue car came speeding and stopped abruptly in front of Amaryllis. Richard stepped out of the car and surprised her and Isabel by pulling out a gun of his own.

"Father help me, she wants to kill me. She's crazy," Amaryllis screamed. Richard rushed to his daughter, shielding her as he aimed his gun at Isabel.

"Drop your gun or I will shoot you," he screamed but Isabel didn't even flinch. She was still aiming her gun at Amaryllis as some of her body was still peeking out from behind her dad's figure.

"No one hurts my daughter," he said as he started pulling the trigger, but Isabel had already fired a bullet at the tiny portion of Amaryllis that managed to peek out from behind her dad's broad figure. Amaryllis screamed in pain and she clutched her shoulder. Falling, she wailed. Richard squinted his eyes and fired three shots at Isabel, but she dropped her body to the ground and the shots hit the door of the house instead. Police sirens sounded nearby and Isabel's body started trembling. Her sweaty palms clutched her gun tighter. Police cars rushed through the gate and came to a stop behind Richard's car, as policemen and policewomen rushed out and surrounded Isabel.

"Abandon your weapon and put your hands above your head," the police demanded. Isabel tossed her gun to the ground, smiling wickedly as her mission was accomplished, or so she had thought. As the police led her to the car in handcuffs, she noticed Amaryllis only had a small wound on her shoulder. She gritted her teeth.

"She's still alive? No," she screamed and struggled against the police' hold as she tried to free herself and finish her job. Richard shouted a couple of curse words at Isabel as the police restrained him from attacking her. Only when Isabel was out of sight, did Richard manage to compose himself. His eyes flashed with panic as he seemed to remember that his daughter was injured. He jumped up and down, waving his hands frantically in the air when he saw the ambulance speeding in.

"Sir calm yourself down. Your daughter will be fine," a policewoman said. Richard grunted in response as he continued his frantic act. Over the next few moments, the police had discovered the wounded maid and she and Amaryllis were lifted onto a stretcher whilst Richard hovered over his daughter, his hands trembling terribly as he ran his hands down the side of her face.

Amaryllis' eyelids fluttered open and she scanned the peculiar place she was in. It was most definitely not her room. She couldn't see her wardrobe or her dressing table. The walls were a light blue and the room was mostly empty, apart from the bed she was sleeping in. She heard a beeping noise and looked up in the direction it was coming from. She saw a strange machine that looked awfully like what she had seen in one of those doctor shows she always binged watched over the weekend.

Then it all came back to her. She remembered the blood, the guns, the police and her wounded shoulder. She had been shot. That means she must be in the hospital. She hoped her dad was okay, but then she remembered the police had caught Isabel before she passed out. Her dad must have come with her in the ambulance and he must be in the hospital. Regardless, she still wanted to make sure her dad was uninjured.

Her prayers were answered as the door opened and her dad and a nurse came in. The nurse smiled warmly as she said her good mornings.

"How is our patient today?" the nurse asked. Her father came up to her, smiling brightly and gave his only daughter a sloppy kiss on the forehead.

"I am fine I just feel a little bit of pain on my shoulder," Amaryllis said.

"Well, that's normal. You seem to be in pretty good health. We will keep you here for one more day and then the doctor will see if we should discharge you home," the nurse said. She gave Amaryllis a dose of her medicine and left shortly after.

"Dad I heard one of the maids scream. I think Isabel shot her," Amaryllis said. Her dad nodded sadly.

"But don't worry she's recovering very fast," her father said. Amaryllis sighed in relief. Shortly after, her father left her to go and get her some of her favourite dessert. She had asked him for a French toast from La Rose and he had been eager to see her bright smile so he all but flew to La Rose. Boredom struck her and she started braiding small sections of her hair after finding nothing else to do. She touched her hair and felt it between her fingers. It had dried now and was a bit of a mess since she didn't have a chance to blow dry it. Opening the braids up, she curled her hair between her fingers, making loose little curls.

Suddenly, the door opened. She craned her neck to see who had come but couldn't see anything. Amaryllis tried to get up but pain shot up her shoulder as soon as she moved her upper body. She was expecting her dad to enter but instead, she saw the last person she wanted to see. Shockingly it wasn't Derek. Or Rose. This woman had tight brown curls falling over her shoulder and eyes that were nearly pitch black. The woman walked towards Amaryllis' bed with a little cute boy on her hips. He was sucking his thumb as he mumbled something Amaryllis couldn't catch, but it sounded like he was saying mummy. Amaryllis tried to sit up on her bed this time, but waves of pain washed over her body once again and she closed her mouth shut to stop her screams from escaping. She hissed in pain and fell back down in a sleeping position.

"You are in pain. Good," the woman said. Amaryllis' eyes enlarged in shock. "You and your daughter are pure evil. This is what you say to me after your daughter tried to kill me." The woman took a few steps closer to her bed.

"She only did that because you left her no choice. You kept going after the man she loves, who by the way, she has a child with," Isabel's mother said as she pointed towards the little boy on her hip. Amaryllis looked at the boy and studied his features. He really did look like a mix between Derek and Isabel. He had Isabel's dark brown hair, but his stunning blue eyes looked nothing like Isabel's black eyes. Amaryllis couldn't believe what she was seeing. The baby's eyes were a replica of Derek's. It was as if Amaryllis was staring into Derek's eyes. Only now did she realise how much she missed staring into his eyes and how much she missed him.

"Even if that's true and this is their child, I already tried to explain to your daughter before she shot me that I wasn't going after Derek. I don't like him anymore. He is the one that keeps coming after me. Every day I discover something new about him and all of those things have been disappointing," Amaryllis said out of breath.

"Because of you my daughter will be put in prison, but you could change that for this child. Look at him, he's so innocent. Do you think he deserves to not be able to see his mother," she said, ignoring whatever Amaryllis said and went straight to the main reason why she was here. Amaryllis narrowed her eyes.

"That's because of the choices your daughter made. There's nothing I can do about it so I don't understand why you are telling me about this," Amaryllis said.

"Yes, you can. If you tell the police that she shot you by mistake, maybe they won't throw her in prison," Isabel's mother sneered. Amaryllis looked taken aback. Her laughs echoed and bounced off the walls. Isabel's mother stared at her in disdain.

"You really are crazy, now I understand where your daughter gets it from. And something else, your daughter also shot one of my maids. So even if I say your daughter shot me by mistake, which the police would never believe, you would have to find another story to cover up her first victim," Amaryllis said. Isabel's mother pursed her lips together and started cursing at Amaryllis.

Just then the door opened again and in came Richard. As soon as he laid eyes on Isabel's mother, his eyes narrowed. He screamed at her to get out and when she protested, he pushed her out and called security.

By the end of the week, everyone at the school had got news of Derek and Isabel's secret son.

Natalie, Lisa and James came to visit Amaryllis in the hospital every day until she got discharged. Derek tried to visit her a few times, but Richard had called security on him.

Kristina had also come to visit Amaryllis a few times and Amaryllis enjoyed her company very much. Kristina was like the sister Amaryllis never had. Although she was twice her age, Kristina was like a teenager at heart. She was so relatable and fun to talk to.

Kristina kept coming to their house to check on Amaryllis as she was a doctor and had volunteered to do the check-ups. She came every week and James and Richard seemed ecstatic with her presence. Lisa however, never left her daughter by herself with 'that woman'. Lisa had told Richard she was convinced Kristina was evil. Richard had laughed at his wife's absurdness, as he usually did whenever Lisa gave her opinion about anything, whether she was being absurd or not. One afternoon, Kristina had finished checking up on Amaryllis and was pouring herself a cup of coffee she had made when James barged into the kitchen.

"How are you doing?" he said smirking. He had his hands in the pockets of his jeans and looked Kristina up and down. She smiled sweetly at him as she sipped her coffee.

"I am okay, how are you?" she said.

"Why do you act as if you don't know me and why do you call yourself Kristina?" he asked, getting straight to the point. Kristina tilted her head with a questioning look flashing in her eyes. James smirked at her, clearly not falling for her innocent act.

"I... I... er I don't know you and my name is Kristina," she tried to say firmly, but it sounded like she was a student with stage fright that had to make a speech in front of the entire school.

"How could you forget? Don't you remember the goods you gave me?" he said, motioning with his hands to his pockets. Kristina nearly dropped her cup. She slammed the cup down and covered James' mouth. She shushed him and looked towards the door to see if anyone had heard what he had said.

"But I didn't expect you to be a doctor, so that's where you steal the drugs from," he said. Kristina shook her head. She told him that it wasn't her and that he had her confused with somebody else. James reached into his pocket and took a little sack out that had a powder in it. Kristina's eyes widened in recognition. She hissed at him to hide it and he tossed it from hand to hand as she tried to grab it from him. When a maid came rushing in, James stuffed the drugs back in his pocket. Kristina and James straightened their posture and Kristina went back to drinking her coffee whilst James made his way out of the kitchen.

Chapter 19

Kidnapped

A week passed by and Amaryllis had completely healed. Richard and Lisa had locked their bickering away in their bedroom, instead of letting it spread around the house as they usually did.

They were getting ready for a meeting at their company. Richard attempted to tie his tie and for once in his life, he had succeeded. Or so he imagined. Lisa took a look at her husband and frowned. Richard's hands fell to his sides and he shrugged. Lisa attempted to untie the mess around his neck. She redid the tie and made a perfect knot. Now his outfit was complete. His outfit consisted of a white shirt tucked into navy trousers, a navy tie and a navy blazer. Lisa smiled proudly at her work and preceded to walk away, but Richard got a hold of her hand. She tilted her head at him quizzically, but when she received no response, she tried to wiggle her hand out of his grasp. However, that deemed impossible since he had an iron grip. She glared at his cold expressionless face. His eyes pierced into hers and she squirmed under his strong gaze. She pulled her hand more strongly this time and this time, he let go. Lisa stumbled backwards, nearly hitting the door.

"Can't a man hold his wife's hand," he said, looking at his wife with innocent eyes. Lisa grumbled something under her breath and went back to her dressing table. She sat down and started curling her short blonde hair.

Richard stood there, staring at her as she curled each strand. His hands were in the pocket of his trousers and he leaned his back against the wall.

Lisa's hand shook with each strand she curled and each time he noticed the effect he had on her, he smiled. Out of the corner of her eyes, she could see his wicked smile spread across his face. Her lower lip trembled, but she sucked in a long breath and calmed her nerves.

"You know what a wife's punishment should be if she was ever caught cheating on her husband?" Richard asked out of the blue, filling the room with added tension. Lisa gulped but continued curling her last few strands.

"No. What should it be?" she asked. Richard glided across the room to her table. Her neck was bare from the side as most of her hair was on the right side, leaving only a few strands sitting on the left. He breathed down her neck as he lowered his head so his lips were right next to her left ear. He spoke his next few words so quietly Lisa thought she must have heard wrong.

"The punishment should be death," he hissed. Lisa dropped her hair curler on the floor as Richard moved away from her. He laughed wickedly as her eyes pricked with tears. She blinked the tears back and retrieved her hair curler. She curled the last strands of her hair, though these last few strands looked more waved than curled due to the severe shaking of her hands.

Putting her curler away, she changed into a sleek black dress. She wrestled with the zipper as it did not want to go up the zipper chain. Richard slapped her hands away from the zipper and zipped the dress up. Lisa flinched. It was as if she was afraid that he would zip her skin with it. She applied her red lipstick as Richard waited for her, like the understanding husband he pretended to be. But he wasn't pretending to be an understanding husband. In fact, he wasn't pretending at all. He was being understanding, but he was being an understanding father. A father who wanted his daughter to see that her parents' relationship was repaired as they left the house together. This whole act was so their daughter would see her mother and father happy together. At least for now whilst she recovered from her wound.

Kristina paced up and down her hotel room. She thought long and hard this past week about her plan. She could not let James tell everyone about her fake name that she used when she used to sell drugs. Otherwise, they would not trust Amaryllis around her. If they did not trust her to spend time with Amaryllis, that meant that she would have to follow her and kidnap her, making her job much harder as she would have to make sure no one sees her illegal act. If she doesn't find an opportunity to kidnap her outside her house, she would have to break into her house. Breaking into her house was next to impossible. Richard had bragged to Kristina about a security system they had in place, that alerted everyone in the house if a thief or any trespasser made it past the gate. That meant that she would be caught by the police, which was the least of her concerns because she expected to be caught sooner or later. However, she could not be caught before she completed her revenge plan, and the first step was to kidnap Amaryllis without anyone knowing.

On the subject of Amaryllis, Kristina had decided that the big day was today. Today was the day she would take Amaryllis to her secret place. It was a small wooden house located in the forest. The forest was filled with wolves and snakes so no one ever dared to go near the area. There they would finally be alone. Kristina knew what part of the forest to stay in to avoid the beasts of nature. She called Amaryllis yesterday and she was more than happy for Kristina to take her to Kristina's favourite Italian Restaurant. At least, that's what Kristina had told her. Kristina was ready for her mission. She wore black leather trousers with a black leather jacket. She wore black shoes and had black gloves inside her pockets.

As soon as she arrived downstairs at the hotel reception, she asked them to bring her car. She put on her gloves and hid her gun in the car. Going inside the car, she felt her stomach start to hurt.

"Ugh not again," she said as she took another ibuprofen tablet. She was on her period and had been getting very bad period cramps. She hoped they wouldn't be too bad because she didn't want to pass out when she was finally this close to avenging her sister. Otherwise, she would have to cancel this plan.

After driving for twenty minutes, she arrived at Amaryllis' house. She should call it a castle. It was at least as big as a castle. Looking at the castle in front of her, Kristina finally understood what her sister liked about Richard. He was rich. Filthy rich. A girl could get everything she ever dreamed of with money like his. All her dreams could become reality with him.

The princess came out of her castle, wearing white trousers and a blue t-shirt which she accessorised with a white shoulder bag and white loafers. Kristina laughed silently. White was such a great choice for today's scheduled events.

"White, white, white, not a good choice for the place you are visiting today," muttered Kristina as she smiled and waved to Amaryllis from her car window. Amaryllis opened the door and hopped in the passenger seat.

"Hello," she said excitedly. Kristina started her car before Amaryllis had managed to put her seat belt on. She sped through the highway and let her happy demeanour change to one of anger.

"I love Italian food. I am so excited to eat there. What's the best thing they have?" Amaryllis asked. No answer. "So, when are we getting there? Is it far?" Kristina flipped her head around and shot Amaryllis a glare.

"What's wrong, are you okay?" she asked.
Amaryllis huffed and rested her head on the car window. For the rest of the car ride, the only sound that could be heard was the sound of the wind.

Pulling up inside the forest, Kristina let the car move in a bit deeper before turning the engine off. Amaryllis looked around confused, she searched for a restaurant but all she saw were trees. This place looked more like a forest than a place for a restaurant.

There were no buildings. There were no other people but them. Amaryllis soon realised they were alone in a forest.

Kristina opened her door and told her to get out, but Amaryllis shook her head vigorously. Kristina dragged her by the arm and threw her out. Amaryllis screeched in pain as she landed on the hard ground. Panic rushed through Amaryllis' body as she realised the reality of the situation. Kristina slammed the car door shut and pulled out a gun. Amaryllis tried to crawl away but Kristina fired a warning shot in the air.

"Don't you dare try to run, otherwise I'll shoot you and I am not like that stupid Isabel; I won't accidentally shoot you in the shoulder. It will be straight to your heart," Kristina said. Amaryllis turned around and stood on her feet. She dusted her white trousers, but it was too late. Just when she thought things couldn't get any worse her favourite trousers were ruined.

"Aw, what's wrong? Are your trousers ruined?" Kristina said. Amaryllis gave her the evil eye.

"Yes, in fact, these were my favourite jeans," she said. Kristina gave her a fake side smile, her expression turning hard. She grabbed her by the arm and led her deeper into the forest. They walked for hours, and every few minutes she used her gun to threaten Amaryllis with death if she ever tried to run.

Finally, they reached their destination. Kristina threw the wooden door open and pushed Amaryllis inside. Amaryllis stumbled and fell on a dirty mattress. Kristina took Amaryllis' bag and pulled out her phone. She opened the camera app.

"Perfect, now I'll send a pic and show your dad what state his beloved daughter is in," she said. Amaryllis crossed her arms and glared at Kristina who just took more pictures from different angles. After several photos, Amaryllis thought she could make use of this moment to practise her poses. She stood up and put one hand on her hip and one hand on her head. She continued making different poses until Kristina stopped taking pictures and shot her a menacing look.

"Do you think this is one of your photoshoots?" she screamed but Amaryllis started posing in different ways again. Kristina's face became red with rage. No matter how much she threatened or screamed at Amaryllis, she kept on doing her silly poses. Kristina had finally had enough and stepped outside the tiny wooden house. She sent the pictures to Richard and looked out for anyone that might potentially be there.

In the past five minutes Amaryllis had peeked through the house window about fifty times, but there was no sign of anyone that could help her. She searched the wooden house for any telephone she could use to call for help or any sharp object she could defend herself with. There was nothing. The only thing she could find was the mattress she fell on. Apart from that, the whole room was empty. There was one small window, but it was made of thick glass and seemed impossible to break. She saw that there must have been a handle that must have been broken as there were remains of something that looked to have been broken on the side of the window. Thus, there was also zero hope of opening the window.

"Are you done exploring your new place?" Kristina said, startling Amaryllis. Kristina walked in as Amaryllis walked to the wall and lowered herself to the ground. She would rather sit on the ground than on that dirty mattress. She stared into nothingness as Kristina watched her reaction to everything.

"Aren't you going to ask me why I have kidnapped you?" Kristina asked.

"There's no point. I've learnt that if people do terrible things, they usually have a stupid reason for it," she said still staring into space.

"I'll tell you anyway," Kristina said and sat across from Amaryllis. Amaryllis' eyes blazed with annoyance and she turned her head around to face the wall. Kristina explained everything to her. How her father had a mistress, who was Ms Emma, who was also Kristina's sister. She also explained to her that Ms Emma was so excited about her relationship with her father and that she used to always tell her about him. She used to describe him as if he was prince charming. She said that he loved her too and that he told her someday he would marry her. She thought she was going to get a fairy-tale ending with him. That she would quit her two jobs that she hated. She thought she would live in a big house with hundreds of maids at her service and not like the small house she lived in.

Suddenly when Kristina was halfway through her story, she heard snoring. She looked up to find Amaryllis fast asleep with drool on the side of her mouth. She smacked her hand on the floor harshly, but Amaryllis' snoring only got louder. Kristina placed both her hands on Amaryllis' shoulders and shook her awake. Amaryllis yelped in surprise.

"Aw Kristina when did you come? Oh, never mind you backstabbing bitch I just remembered that you kidnapped me," she said, her face going from genuinely happy to genuinely angry. Kristina raised her hand and tried to strike her but Amaryllis moved her head back faster than light travels.

"As I was saying, your father promised to marry my sister and then he backed out for you. The only way to punish him is to kill you since you're the only person he loves, " she said. Amaryllis mastered a bored expression as she put her hand under her chin.

"How's this my father's fault? It's not like your sister decided to kill herself because she was so sad that my father would not marry her," Amaryllis said in her most dramatic voice and mockingly put her hand around her throat in a choking hold. Kristina clenched her teeth and her jaw tightened.

"My sister died because Mr Andrews shot her because he blamed her for the police catching and putting him in prison," Kristina blurted out all in one go. Amaryllis stared at Kristina with a blank expression on her face, not being able to connect the dots. She threw her hands in the air exasperatedly.

"I still don't understand how this is my father's fault," she said.

"It's his fault because my sister had hired Mr Andrews to kill you. However, when he got caught by the police, he killed my sister because she was the one that told him and paid him to shoot you," she said. Amaryllis took a moment to process the huge dump of information Kristina had thrown at her. She then preceded to gape at Kristina.

"Are you kidding me. That maniac was about to kill me and the entire class, and instead of apologising for what your maniac sister did, you blame my father for her death and want to kill me for it. She had it coming," Amaryllis said. Kristina stood up and pulled her gun out, aiming it at Amaryllis' head. Amaryllis raised her hands in surrender and told her to calm down.

"Don't you ever call my sister crazy," she said.

"I called her a maniac not crazy. Are you hearing things now, are you going cr-" Amaryllis was cut off by the gun releasing a bullet that hit the wall. If she measured the distance between her head and the bullet, she would find that it was exactly one centimetre away from its target. Amaryllis' lower lip trembled and Kristina looked at her as if she was challenging her to speak.

"Lisa, Lisa," Richard screamed as he went downstairs. Lisa was sitting in the living room, reading a fashion magazine. She pretended she could not hear her abusive husband and flipped to the next page. She had spent her whole day with him today and had hoped she would have the rest of her evening free of him. She wanted to relax - emotionally and physically. Alas, some wishes were not granted. Richard rushed into the living room, panting, his face drained from all colour. She spared a glance at him and then glanced back at her magazine. He stormed up to her and grabbed her magazine, throwing it on the floor. She protested and cursed under her breath. She really didn't want to fight with him. Richard put his phone in front of Lisa's face. Yanking his phone from him, her eyes glued to the mesmerising picture in front of her. She looked at the rare gem in awe. It was a beautiful diamond necklace with many green emeralds decorating it. Not that it needed decoration. This was by far the most beautiful necklace Lisa had ever seen in her entire life and it was much more beautiful than the cheap silver necklaces Richard bought her for their anniversary every year. The ones he claimed were expensive diamond necklaces in front of his precious daughter.

"What a beautiful diamond. Are you buying this for me?" she said.

"What the hell are you talking about? Are you seriously talking about diamonds when our daughter has been kidnapped?" Richard said and snatched the phone from her hand. He looked at the picture she had been looking at and saw the picture of the diamond necklace he had wanted to buy for Kristina. Though in his defence, that was before she kidnapped his only daughter. He must have accidentally opened the photos app.

He took the picture of Amaryllis out and showed it to his wife. It took her forever to focus on the background in the picture and notice the messages Kristina had sent him. Her eyes scanned through the messages and they flickered with shock instead of excitement this time as she looked at her daughter's dirty clothes and her tired face.

"How dare she kidnap her? What does she want with her? This is all your fault. I told you there was something weird about that woman," she said and pounded her fists on his chest. Richard slumped down on the sofa, a look of defeat appearing on his facial features. Lisa kept screaming and blaming him as he read over the messages Kristina had sent him. She had not asked for money. She had not asked for anything. Richard was more confused than he had ever been in his life. For once in his life, he felt powerless. He didn't know what to do. There was only one thing he could do – call the police, and so that's what he did.

Chapter 20

Wolves

Amaryllis' eyes fluttered open. Direct sunlight blinded her and she shut her eyelids tightly and turned her head around to face the wall. She sat up on the cold hard ground and her eyes scanned the place she was in. She was in a very empty and cold place. There was no furniture or anything else there other than a dirty mattress.

All of a sudden, all the memories came rushing back to her. She remembered how Kristina had kidnapped her. How she had held her captive in this wooden house, in the middle of nowhere. How she had tried shooting her. And how she had told her all about Ms Emma. Her head spun with the information rushing to her head all at once. She held her head as it started to ache.

No later than a few moments after Amaryllis woke up, the door to the wooden house was kicked open. In came Kristina, the same Kristina that two days ago Amaryllis loved and found to be the most interesting person she had ever met. Now she was just a devil in her eyes.

"Why haven't you killed me yet? What are you waiting for?" Amaryllis said whilst glaring daggers at Kristina. Kristina hummed as she glided across the room and grabbed Amaryllis from the collar of her t-shirt. Amaryllis' feet hung in the air as Kristina held her up above the ground. She kicked her feet at Kristina, but could not reach her since Kristina held her in distant proximity. Amaryllis' first instinct that Kristina was strong was right. She had immediately paid attention to her muscly arms when she had first seen her.

"I am waiting for your parents to do whatever they can do to save you; I want to see them run around like donkeys and think they can save their daughter. I want them to be in despair but still have hope left, and then I will kill you," Kristina spat. Amaryllis' eyes glistened with fear and she gulped. This woman was not just a devil, she was evil itself. She relished in the torture of others. She relished in the despair of Amaryllis, who was scared alone in a forest. She relished in the despair of Amaryllis' parents, who were sitting and waiting for the police to call them, watching their phones, their eyes unblinking. Kristina let go of Amaryllis, letting her fall to the ground with a loud thud. Amaryllis grunted in pain as she clutched her left leg. Kristina gave her a disgusted look and for once Amaryllis mirrored her emotions. She was disgusted by her. She was not the charming confident woman that Amaryllis aspired to be like. She was an ugly evil witch that Amaryllis wanted to run away from. Kristina shot her one last dirty look before leaving the abandoned house and locking the door behind her.

Hours must have passed by whilst Amaryllis sat there massaging her leg, hoping to numb the pain. She also played with her hair and made braids to distract herself from the pain and the boredom. The only interesting thing Amaryllis had was her view of the moon. The moon had made an appearance in the sky. It was nearly a full moon again. It was magnificent. It glowed like a thousand stars and brightened up the sky. It was truly a source of light in the darkness. Amaryllis looked at the moon in hope and prayed. She prayed she would be free. That God would help her. Although there was no possible way out, she decided to have faith that she would be free. She had faith she would get out of this hellhole. She closed her eyes and prayed one last time before the sound of lightning startled her.

Her eyes flipped open like a light switch and that's when she saw the lightning hit the window and shatter the glass into a thousand pieces. There was still some glass left where the window had been, but as the second wave of lightning struck it, there was no glass left as the rest of it shattered to the ground. It was a true miracle. It was like the lightning was specifically targeting the glass on the window. Amaryllis rushed to the window and started climbing over it. She put one of her legs over it and that's when she heard the jiggling of keys. She hurriedly put her other leg over and jumped out the window. She crouched down, and in that position, she walked around the house until she reached the corner. She walked away from the corner of the house and to the direction of the trees, still bent down so her head wasn't sticking out and nobody would see her.

That nobody was Kristina. Kristina entered the house; her eyes scanned the room before landing on the shattered window. She cursed under her breath. "That brat," she screamed as she rushed out the door, prompting Amaryllis to run as fast as she had in her life into the forest. She ran for her life, knowing very well that if she was ever caught by Kristina, she would make her meet her maker.

The chilling night air froze her body to the core. It was as if it was already wintering in this forest.

Amaryllis saw pure darkness as her feet ran without anything to guide them. She felt herself step on some leaves and mud and soon the rain started pouring down. Her left leg still throbbed and she knew that soon she would have to stop and rest. Her leg would not be able to take much more pressure. The rain poured down like a waterfall and made the ground even muddier. Her feet glided on the mud like a ballerina glides across the dance floor. Her feet felt like they were walking on ice and she slid. She tried to regain her balance and put her arms out, as if that would somehow help. Surprisingly, she regained her balance. After a few moments of looking like someone learning how to ice skate, the mud path ended and she stepped on the grass.

She saw the moon behind the trees and it gave her a bit of light so she could make out the path in front of her. She only prayed Kristina couldn't see the moon and was in complete darkness. But Kristina did have her phone and she could easily use the flashlight. Kristina definitely had an advantage over her.
Amaryllis secretly hoped she had been struck by lightning.

A howl snapped her out of her dark thoughts. She stopped running and looked around. That sound could only mean one thing. Wolves. There were wolves nearby. She searched around the forest and looked between the trees but saw nothing. Then she saw it. A shadow at the top of a cliff. The cliff was not that far away from her. The shadow resembled a wolf figure and now Amaryllis was sure she was doomed. There was no way she could outrun a wolf.

Kristina, yes.

A wolf, no.

She had to run in a different direction but that would mean she would run back to Kristina. But if she continued, she would be eaten by wolves. Her feet made a move as if by their own accord and she found herself running onwards. She would probably die either way. She would rather die by getting eaten by wolves than let that disgusting woman be satisfied that she had killed her to avenge her maniac sister. If anything, Amaryllis should be the one to avenge herself by going after Kristina after what Ms Emma made her go through her, but Amaryllis didn't blame innocent people for the crimes others committed.

"Amaryllis stop running. You won't get away. I will catch you eventually and if I don't, the wolves will catch you. And if the wolves catch you, they will eat you. If you come back, I promise I will reconsider killing you," she heard Kristina say. She sounded out of breath. Amaryllis sighed in relief. Amaryllis was not an idiot. She knew Kristina would never spare her life. She saw too much hatred when she looked into her eyes. Kristina's blue eyes seemed black with darkness and her hatred for Amaryllis would never allow her to spare her life. Amaryllis had to bite her tongue to stop herself from shouting back that she would rather be eaten by wolves than go back to her. But then Kristina would know where she is.

Suddenly, Amaryllis got an idea. She would hide behind a tree, wait for Kristina to run past her and then make her way back to the house. Then from there, she would run back from where they had first come from. That way she would avoid the wolves and maybe she could survive.

Amaryllis' wide smile dropped as she stared at the creature in front of her. It was too late. A monstrous creature on all fours was now growling at her. He stood a few feet away from her. His teeth were like sharp fangs and he looked at her like a piece of huge meat. She put her arms up as if the wolf would understand she meant no harm. The wolf wasn't the police. She took a few steps back but the wolf stayed in place. Amaryllis decided to be brave and try to walk around the wolf.

Big mistake.

The wolf growled at her and howled. Soon she heard the rest of his pack coming. She heard more howling and heavier footsteps coming closer. After a few more howls and growls she was surrounded by wolves. She looked from one wolf to the other, hoping to see if there was one that was weak that she could escape through, but they all looked like wild beasts.

To her surprise, a shot sounded in the air. The wolves backed a few feet away from Amaryllis but still growled at her. Another shot sounded and one of the wolves yelped. Blood gushed from his leg and this time they all ran away.

"I will kill you, you little brat, if it's the last thing I do," Kristina said, sounding closer than Amaryllis liked to believe she was. Amaryllis made a run for it as the branches of the trees hit her face and body. She shoved them away but more attacked her. She shoved them away again and ran faster than her left leg could take. After an hour of running, shoving branches out of her way, tripping and falling on things she couldn't properly see, she finally made it to a street. She could see a car approaching with blinding lights and she waved her hands and ran into the street. She jumped up and down frantically. She must have looked out of her mind.

"Hello, help me please," she begged. To her surprise, the car stopped and she saw that it was a police car. Perfect.

"Are you Amaryllis Knight?" a policeman asked as he stepped out of the car. He looked worriedly at her as he drew his gun out and put it to his side.

She must have looked horrific. Her hair was a mess and it looked like a nest. It was decorated with leaves and sticks, whilst her white trousers looked more black than white. Her blue shirt was worn and torn, exposing one of her shoulders and making her look more like a homeless person than someone that had been kidnapped.

She nodded vigorously at the officer's question. She looked down, not feeling her legs. She found herself slowly falling to her knees. She panted heavily, her chest rising and falling. She sat on the ground as the officer opened the car door. Amaryllis' ears perked up as she heard leaves rustling and tree branches moving. The rain and wind had stopped and the air had no movement in it whatsoever. It was still, dead almost. She turned her head around and saw a figure approaching her from the forest with a gun aimed at her. Amaryllis somehow managed to stand up and scream. The police officer drew his gun and pointed it at Kristina.

"You will pay for the death of my sister," she hissed as she pulled the trigger and fired a shot at the same moment Amaryllis ran towards the police car. The police officer fired a shot at Kristina but she had already started her escape. The policeman's shot hit a tree, whilst Kristina's shot hit its target. Amaryllis put her hand on her chest. Blood soaked her blue t-shirt and horrific pain surged through her body. Her body shook violently. She looked around; her eyes blazed with pure fear. She wondered if this was how her life would end.

Then, her life started flashing before her eyes. She saw herself standing outside of the guest room in her house where she had first witnessed her mother's infidelity. She saw herself fighting with Rose over Derek. She saw Nicholas telling her about the bet and she saw many more images that kept rushing through her mind. They kept attacking her mind. At this point she was not sure which was more painful, the physical or the emotional pain.

"Hey stay with me, don't close your eyes, the ambulance is on the way," the policeman said as he hovered over Amaryllis.

The familiar sound of the beeping monitor was the first thing Amaryllis heard. As soon as she opened her eyes, she felt excruciating pain coming from her chest.

"Hey, how are you feeling?" a voice asked her. Natalie was staring down at her with her big blue eyes. Amaryllis didn't have the energy to put on a fake smile or pretend that she was okay. She had been shot. Twice. Both times were because of what others had done. First Derek and now her father. What her father had done was unforgivable. He had cheated on her mother. She felt shameful that she treated her mother so badly when for years her father was the one cheating on her mother. Only now did she understand what her mother had meant. The only reason she had cheated was because she probably knew he was cheating on her. She probably felt it.

Natalie dragged a chair to her bedside and sat down. She took her hand in hers and gave it a gentle squeeze. For a while, Natalie just sat there, not saying anything. It was quiet and peaceful and Amaryllis liked this atmosphere, but it wouldn't last long.

Amaryllis' head whipped around as the door was thrown open and in entered her father, mother and uncle. Her mother threw herself at her daughter and hugged her. Amaryllis whimpered in pain and her mother drew back. Her uncle bent down and kissed her, and for the first time in months, she smiled at him. He seemed surprised but returned her smile. Her father stood there, silently looking at his daughter with tears brimming his eyes. Amaryllis shook her head in disappointment.

"My baby girl," he cried out and leaned down to kiss her. Amaryllis was not bothered to put up a fight and let him kiss her. He pulled out a napkin and wiped his tears. Seconds later, a doctor came in and told them that she needed to rest. Amaryllis felt her whole body relax as she saw them all leave. She really wanted to be alone right now.

A knock came on the door and before she could say enter, the person had already let himself in. A policeman came in. She thought he seemed familiar and then recognised him as the policeman that saved her from the devil. He approached her bed and took a seat on the chair.

"Good morning. I have good news for you," he said. "You don't have to worry about Kristina anymore because she's dead. She fell off a cliff as police were chasing after her in the forest. Amaryllis stared at him wide-eyed but then sighed. Finally, she was safe. She wasn't going to lie or pretend that she was sad about Kristina falling off a cliff. She deserved it. If Amaryllis was being honest, she deserved much more than that.

"I am really relieved. I am just curious how you found me so quickly," she said.

"Your phone had your location on it. Kristina forgot to turn your location off from your phone and so the police used his phone to find you," he said. The policeman bid his farewells and left. Just as Amaryllis was about to close her eyes for some much-needed rest, the door burst open. She grumbled angrily. Blonde curls ran into the room and Natalie slumped in the chair beside her.

"I had to sneak past so many doctors and nurses to get to you. How do you feel?" she said. She stopped her mumbling when she saw the annoyed look on Amaryllis' face. She blushed and looked down at her hands.

"Sorry I will go, you look like you want to take a nap," Natalie apologised. Amaryllis nodded. Natalie's phone rang, making her stare at the screen weirdly. Amaryllis poked her hand and asked her what was wrong.

"Oh, it's nothing. It's just that your mother is calling me. She called me twice half an hour after we left you, but when I answered she didn't say anything and now she's calling again," Natalie said. She moved her finger across the screen, accepting the call. She raised the phone to her right ear and greeted Lisa excitedly, but frowned when she heard a scream from the other side of the line.

"Richard please don't kill him, he's your brother," Natalie heard Lisa cry. Natalie's forehead creased. She felt her breath hitch and her heart slam against her chest. She tried to stop her hands from shaking but they shook even more. She noticed Amaryllis was observing her reaction. She pondered what she would tell Amaryllis but then decided she would settle with a basic lie. She lied to her and told her that Lisa was still not saying anything and rushed out, running faster than a cheetah. Amaryllis' gaze followed Natalie. Her gaze was filled with worry. She wondered what more could happen to her. How could things possibly get worse? She had been shot twice. The first time it was just a small wound to her shoulder, but the second time she was near the brink of death. Maybe she would need to be shot a third time for the universe to decide that she had suffered enough. She selfishly wished all the things that happened to her to happen to anybody else instead. Anybody that she didn't love. Anybody that wasn't her parents, her uncle or Natalie. She wanted to be free. Free from pain. Free from suffering. She wanted to go back to how her life used to be a few months ago. It wasn't perfect. Her parents were always fighting, but at least no one was trying to kill her.

Chapter 21

All Alone

    With a big stick in one hand and a gun in another Richard peered down at James. He was laying on the floor, blood pooled down from his nose and mouth as he wheezed. His body shook and he used his hands to try and get up, but every time he tried he fell on his stomach. His white shirt was stained red.

    Lisa sat in front of Richard on a chair, her hands were tied behind her back. Red lines could be seen forming on her wrists. Her eyes were red and her cheeks had some residue of tear droplets that hadn't dried yet.

There were no windows in the abandoned building Richard had bought them to and the ceiling was so high and the walls were so dark one would think they were in an abandoned castle. The place had nothing in it but two chairs.

Lisa peered down at James as he continued coughing out more blood. Richard watched his younger brother with no hint of regret in his eyes.
In fact, there was no emotion in his eyes whatsoever. His eyes looked empty and dark, as if they reflected death itself. He turned to Lisa and a look of disgust replaced his dullness. Lisa flinched and screamed as he started to move towards her. She tried to run away but the only thing she managed to do was to make her chair shake. She had forgotten she was restrained to a chair. Red lines formed around her ankles as the thick
rope stretched from her sudden movements. Richard stopped a few feet away from her as if he was afraid of getting too close to her.

"Please let us go, please for Amaryllis," she begged. An emotion flickered through Richard's eyes. For a moment only the silence could be heard,
then Richard dropped his gun and stick to the floor. Lisa sighed, a smile stretching across her face.

"Thank y-" she said but a hard slap landing across her face cut her off. A red mark formed on her cheeks as her blonde hair fell over her face. He gripped her chin and forced her to face him.

"Don't you dare say my daughter's name. You are filthy and I don't want you to dirty her name. If you cared about her even a little bit then you would have spent time with her and got to know her, but the only thing you did was fight with her daily. If you cared about her, you certainly wouldn't have cheated on her father," he boomed and raised his hand for another slap. His hand came in contact with Lisa's cheek for the fifth time today.

"I do care about her. She's my daughter, not yours," she screamed at him. It was as if time had stopped. It was as if the universe had frozen still. Richard stood frozen like a statue, not even a finger moving. It had been more than a few minutes and his eyes hadn't even blinked. Lisa looked at him fearfully. As Richard was busy freezing still, James had mastered the remaining strength he had left and managed to get up.

"What do you mean she's not mine?" he said almost so lowly it was like a whisper. It was as if he was afraid of hearing the answer. The one genuine and pure thing in his life that he had was his love for his daughter. If she wasn't his he would lose his love for her. If he lost it, he would have nothing. Nothing in his life would have meaning. Nothing in his life had meaning anyway. Apart from Amaryllis. Richard grabbed Lisa by the hair.

"What do you mean she's not mine?" he repeated his question. Lisa wailed out in pain and bit her lower lip as Richard dragged her hair harder. Suddenly Richard was pushed to the floor. James wrestled him down on the floor as they rolled away from Lisa, both punching each other and kicking each other like two dogs rolling down a hill. Lisa screamed whenever Richard landed a punch on James and cheered whenever James landed a punch on Richard. But Richard was bigger and stronger and had the upper hand. He landed eighty per cent of the punches and James' pale face was now fully red. It looked like he had decided to paint his entire face red to pose as the devil on Halloween. Whenever James tried to punch Richard, he missed and punched the floor instead. He yelped in pain as his fist collided with the floor and the sound of bones breaking alerted the trio to the fact that his knuckles had broken. Richard seemed to have control of the situation once again as he knocked James unconscious and dragged him to another chair next to Lisa. He tied his hands and feet with a thick rope. He then picked up a water bottle from the floor and opened the lid. He threw the contents of the bottle at James' face. The blood started washing down from his face and went on his shirt. His nose was still bleeding, coating his mouth and chin with the red liquid. James woke up with a startle. He gasped as he sucked a breath in as if he had been swimming underwater for a while.

"Leave him alone. You have already hurt him enough," Lisa begged. Richard threw the bottle aside and crouched down next to Lisa.

"You know he's just as stupid as you. The gun and stick were right there and yet he didn't take any of them. Similarly, you chose the poor brother instead of the rich one that took care of you and your horrible spendings all these years," he sneered. Lisa rolled her eyes.

"You always bring that up. If you wanted a woman that didn't like fashion and expensive things as much as I did then why didn't you marry someone else. I'll tell you why," she said. Richard's eyes bore into hers and an intrigued look crossed his face.

"Because I used to date your brother and you knew that. That's why you wanted me. You wanted everything he ever had," she said. This time Richard didn't feel like a slap across the face would express his feelings so he drew his hand back and formed a fist. He quickly pulled it towards Lisa's face and it collided with her mouth. Lisa fell back with her chair and she screeched as blood poured from her mouth. She spit the blood out and licked her lips.

"You still didn't answer me. What do you mean Amaryllis is not my daughter?" he asked for the hundredth time. Lisa started laughing hysterically and with each laugh, she coughed more blood out.

"She's not yours, she's James'," she said. Richard stared at the woman whom he had once loved with betrayed eyes. He breathed heavily and put his fist in his mouth. He grunted loudly and tried not to burst out screaming.

"She's really mine?" James grunted from the other chair with one of his eyes open. Lisa nodded.

"Shut up. You are both liars. Amaryllis is my daughter," Richard said whilst James snickered.

"She's mine, she's mine, your daughter is mine," James sang. Richard stopped for a second and for the first time in a long time, a wave of calmness washed over him.

"She's mine," he finally said and Lisa shook her head vigorously. He nodded just as vigorously as she had shaken her head, but Lisa shook her head again. James watched their exchange with tired eyes.

"Yes, she's mine. That's why you hate her. You've always hated her. You've always fought with her. You used to always find something to fight with her over. She could be sitting down with us at dinner and you would start an argument about how she left a few broccoli pieces uneaten, although you know she hates broccoli," he said as he crouched down next to Lisa. Lisa sniffed and wailed.

"I thought you said she was mine. And I actually believed you," James said and gave her the evil eye. Sobs rocked Lisa's body as Richard stood up and walked to his dear brother. He gave him a once over and then raised his fist up. James shut his eyes closed. But the punch never came. He opened his eyes to see Richard staring at him with a look of disgust. He walked away and picked his gun from the floor.

"Since you two love each other so much I am sure it will be very hard for you to choose which one of you will live," he said and Lisa and James looked at each other, shock embedded in their features. Richard chuckled.

"I will kill one of you today and the other I will set free. But you have to choose. When I count to three you have to choose which one of you will live," he said. They both gulped and pretended to be in deep thought. Lisa shot James a glare but he looked away. Richard started to count to three and when he got to two, they both said their name. Richard laughed maniacally as they both turned their heads to glare at each other.

"Such true love. Such a strong bond," Richard said. "Tell me my love, was it worth it to ruin our relationship for someone you didn't even care about." Lisa looked at him, her eyes flashing with disdain.

"You always flirted with other women and I am perfectly sure that you have cheated on me more than once so don't pretend like you are an angel," she bit back. Richard rolled his eyes and pointed the gun at her head. She gasped, her bloody teeth coming on display.

"I will kill both of you tonight. I was just playing a little game to show the both of you each other's true colours," he said. Lisa squirmed and moved around in her chair as Richard started pulling the trigger. She moved her head from left to right and every time she moved Richard readjusted his aim. He grunted and he glided along the floor and put the gun on the side of her head. Lisa closed her eyes tightly and started crying. Richard looked at the wall behind him and pulled the trigger. A shot sounded through the abandoned building. It echoed through the place and bounced off the walls, making Richard and James hear the gunshot more than twice. James stared at the wall in front of him as Lisa's lifeless body became still in her chair and her hands dropped to her sides. Richard checked for a pulse against her neck and sighed. She was finally dead. He was finally free of her.

He wondered why he felt so bad. After all, he knew he had given Lisa what she deserved and that's exactly what he was planning to do to his brother. He walked over to his brother. He placed the gun at the same place he did on Lisa's head and started pulling the trigger.

"Wait," James said, making Richard stop. His brother's bloodshot eyes looked into his.

"Please don't kill me. Think about Amaryllis. She would hate you if she knew you killed me. Don't you know how much she loves me," James said. Richard scoffed.

"You think I haven't realised how cold and distant she has been with you. I know that she knows about the affair. She hates you now. Both of you. If I kill you, she won't shed a tear," Richard said and placed the gun on James' head. James started wailing like a baby and his eyes became glossy.

"Shut up. Stop being a baby," he said and held the gun more firmly. He started pulling the trigger again but then stopped when he heard police sirens. James stopped his wailing and listened for the sirens. A smile stretched across his bloody face. Richard looked at his brother, a wicked grin plastered across his face. James watched his brother, a quizzical look on his face.

"Too late," he said and before James could comprehend what he meant, Richard shot him in the head. James' eyes became lifeless and Richard shut his eyelids. The smile Richard had on his face disappeared as quickly as it appeared. Richard raised the gun and pointed it at his head. He had lived enough and now it was time to say goodbye to this cruel world.

"Goodbye my beautiful daughter," Richard said and his sweaty hand pulled the trigger. A third shot left the gun and his body fell to the ground and his gun fell next to him. He laid there next to Lisa and James, lifeless and unmoving.

Amaryllis sat up in her bed. Her head hurt and she tried to fix her eyes on a particular object in the room, but they couldn't focus on anything and the room didn't stop spinning. She gripped the sides of her hospital bed, afraid of falling off it. She decided to lay back down.

"Hey how are you doing?" she heard a familiar voice say. She looked up to see Derek. She wondered when he had got here. She had just been looking at the door a few moments ago but did not see anyone come in.

"Where is everyone? Where is Natalie? My parents? Why haven't they come to visit me? It's been two whole days," she complained. Derek looked away from her intense gaze. He rubbed the back of his neck, something he tended to do when he became anxious. Amaryllis looked at him, waiting for an answer but she received nothing. Not even a lie.

Suddenly the door was torn open and Natalie came in panting, her body dripping with sweat. She looked like she had run a marathon.

"It's okay. I am here for you and Derek is here for you too. You will never be alone," Natalie said as she stopped near Amaryllis' bed and took her hands in hers.

Amaryllis looked at her with a funny look on her face. Natalie's face dropped as she shot Derek an annoyed look. Amaryllis wasn't quite sure what the look meant.

"I didn't get a chance to tell her. I just came," he said and Natalie narrowed her eyes at him.

"Guys, what's wrong? Tell me," Amaryllis begged. She started feeling her anxiety levels rise. She had already woken up today after having a horrible nightmare that she couldn't remember. She spent her entire morning trying to remember it but she couldn't remember a thing. She had a feeling it was something to do with her mother cheating on her father but she wasn't sure. The only thing she was sure about was that she was furious. Furious that her father, mother and uncle hadn't visited her. Even Natalie hadn't bothered to check in on her in two days. It was as if they had forgotten about her. As soon as she opened her eyes in the morning, she expected them to be there, but they were not. She wondered where else they could be. Nothing could be more important than her after she was shot for the second time and was on the verge of dying.

"Amaryllis just remember we are always here for you and that you are a strong woman. You can face anything," Derek began and placed his hand on hers. Amaryllis shoved his hand away, starting to get irritated.

"Tell me what's wrong already," she screamed. Natalie and Derek looked at each other as if they were contemplating whether to tell her or not. They knew they didn't have a choice. Sooner or later Amaryllis would know everything. If they didn't tell her the police would or she would receive a call from one of her family members. It was better that they told her everything.

"Your parents and your uncle..." Natalie said but then trailed off. Amaryllis threw her hands up in exasperation.

"Just tell me what happened," she said, getting more irritated as more time was ticking by and she was clearly in the dark about something big that had happened. Natalie gulped but decided to continue.

"They, they were all buried this morning. We attended the funeral. They are all...dead," she finished. Amaryllis stifled a laugh whilst looking at Natalie, who just gave her a sympathetic look. Amaryllis' expression went from amusing to sad to shocked in a matter of seconds.

"No, no, no they were here next to me two days ago and they looked fine," she said. Derek ran his hand down his face.

"I know it's hard to believe but it's true," he said. Amaryllis felt tears prickle in her eyes. She blinked them back and tried to get out of bed but Derek pushed her back gently.

"How did they die? Kristina killed them, didn't she? Wait, isn't Kristina dead?" she sniffed. Derek took a deep breath and decided to be brave.

"Your dad killed your mother and uncle and then shot himself," Derek said. Natalie nudged him harshly.

"You can't tell her all of that in one go," she hissed. Amaryllis stared at them, her pupils flared and realisation washed over her face. That meant her father knew about their affair. How dare he kill her mother and her uncle. He was the one that had been cheating for years.

"The police don't know why he did that but..." Derek trailed off.

"I know why," Amaryllis said.

THE END

Printed in Great Britain
by Amazon